TO THOSE GODS BEYOND

Atlas Anti-Classics 24

GIORGIO MANGANELLI

•

TO THOSE GODS BEYOND

PRECEDED BY

LITERATURE AS DECEPTION

TRANSLATED AND INTRODUCED BY JOHN WALKER

AFTERWORD BY ALASTAIR BROTCHIE

FOREWORD BY

ITALO CALVINO

TRANSLATED BY MARTIN McLAUGHLIN

•

ATLAS PRESS LONDON

Published by Atlas Press, BCM Atlas Press, London WC1N 3XX.
©2019, Atlas Press.
Agli dèi ulteriori by Giorgio Manganelli:
©1989 Adelphi Edizioni S.P.A Milano.
Translation ©2019 John Walker.
(Untitled) blurb for Giorgio Manganelli's *Agli dèi ulteriori* by Italo Calvino:
©The Estate of Italo Calvino, 2002,
used by permission of The Wylie Agency (UK) Limited.
Translation ©2019 Martin McLaughlin.
(Untitled) blurb for the first edition of *Agli dèi ulteriori* by Giorgio Manganelli
published with the permission of the heir to the estate of Giorgio Manganelli.
Introduction ©2019 John Walker.
Afterword ©2019 Alastair Brotchie.
A CIP catalogue for this book is available from the British Library.
ISBN 978-1-900565-81-3.
Printed and bound by CPI, Chippenham.
UK distribution by Turnaround: www.turnaround-uk.com
USA distribution by Artbook/DAP: www.artbook.com

We are extremely grateful to the Istituto Italiano di Cultura di Londra.
This book has been translated thanks to a translation grant awarded by the
Italian Ministry of Foreign Affairs and International Cooperation.
*Questo libro è stato tradotto grazie ad un contributo alla traduzione assegnato dal
Ministero degli Affari Esteri e della Cooperazione Internazionale italiano.*

The cover is from Giovanni Piranesi's engraving *The Outlet of Lake Albano*,
the endpapers are modified versions of *The End (Back into Nothingness)*,
an etching by Max Klinger.

INTRODUCTION

John Walker

●

Giorgio Manganelli was born in Rome in 1922 and died in Milan in 1990. He published a large number of books of fiction, poetry and drama, along with works of criticism, journalism and travel literature; he also published numerous translations from English, including Poe's *Tales of Mystery and Imagination*,[1] and works by Henry James, R.L. Stevenson and Ronald Firbank. He acted as an editorial consultant for some of Italy's major publishers, and was a professor of English literature at the University of Rome. In 1979 Manganelli received the prestigious Viareggio Prize for his *Centuria* (1979).

Manganelli was a significant figure in Gruppo 63, a small association of avant-garde intellectuals which also included Umberto Eco and Eduardo Sanguineti, although he was sceptical about some of the members' radical political and social goals.[2] Unlike the Futurists, Gruppo 63 never produced an actual manifesto and it is thus not possible to give a definitive account of their objectives, especially since former members have given different accounts of the manner in which the group operated. Sanguineti, a member of the Italian Communist Party, inevitably viewed literature from a Marxist perspective, while the primary interest of another member, Angelo Guglielmi, was in linguistic experimentation. While Guglielmi saw literature as contributing to social change, Manganelli's prime concern lay in a subtler subversion, in demonstrating the role language plays in shaping our worlds, and in undermining the discourse of ideologies. Gruppo 63 was to some extent an open group, so Manganelli's focus on language and the creation of experimental fiction was not necessarily at odds with its informal ethos.[3]

In Italy Manganelli is regarded today as a leading figure of the Italian avant-garde, the author who continued to write experimental fiction rather than return to realism. There is a considerable body of critical work on him in Italian and German, and a major study in English.[4] His first work *Hilarotragoedia* (1964) was enthusiastically received by Calvino, an enthusiasm he also extended to *Agli dèi ulteriori* (1972). Calvino regarded Manganelli as a completely original artist, "an irresistible and inexhaustible inventor of games with language and ideas". He wrote the foreword to the first edition of *Agli dèi ulteriori*, and analysed his earlier *Nuovo commento* (1969) in a letter to its author. He compared Manganelli with Swift: "a Swift who allows his saturnalian humour and obsessions to have the most extreme consequences". Manganelli's version of the avant-garde, though primarily involved in the debates of the day about language and the role of literature, is also in part a re-creation of the literary baroque, and incorporates the influence of horror and fantasy writers, such as Poe, H.P. Lovecraft and Stevenson.

Manganelli's text "Literature as Deception" (*La Letteratura come menzogna*, literally "Literature as Lying"), which precedes the novel here, can be regarded as a quasi-manifesto for the Italian neo-avant-garde, with its echoes of Marinetti's *Futurist Manifesto* of 1909, but pertains particularly to Manganelli's own approach to writing, and makes a considerable contribution to our understanding of the main text here, *To Those Gods Beyond*. The argument develops through elaborate and startling metaphors, and an accumulation of paradoxes, in a style that blends pedantry with the poetic. The humanist view of literature comes under sustained attack, coupled to a disdain for the concept of political engagement. The writer is not a noble figure working for the salvation of the world, but merely a buffoon, a prisoner of language itself, and almost its victim. Writing is seen as a solipsistic act, where the writer has only a partial knowledge of what he is creating, for a public that does not exist, a readership of impossible readers.

Language itself forms the substance of the world in which the writer exists, "the only condition which is stable and real, although actually it is unreal and impermanent", in which verbal games, neologisms, extensive alliterations and startling imagery, paradoxes and metamorphoses are an integral part of both the literary "object" and a world whose purpose it is to be literary. Manganelli's conclusion touches on themes and ideas found throughout his work: the idea of literature as a pseudo-mythology which exists in a polytheistic universe, imbued with the gods of the past and assembled by means of symbolic codes such as heraldry and figures of speech, but which is at the mercy of chance, caught up in verbal labyrinths and a landscape of infernos within the cities of the underworld.

To Those Gods Beyond comprises six parts, which Calvino thought to be "profoundly unified", an observation which seems entirely justified despite narrative approaches that include monologues, exchanges of letters between well-known figures from literature, a pedantic essay and introspective narrative voices where the division between being alive and being dead is constantly dissolving. The relationship between its separate elements is achieved through a subtle linking of words or concepts which are subsequently developed at greater length, but also perhaps by something else.

The first two sections consist of dramatic monologues in which the narrators address the reader directly and our understanding is limited to the protagonist's perspective. "A King", which opens the work, displays a series of variations on what appears to be the theme of megalomania, where the king's power is infinite, while in "Simulations" the narrator's ability to invent or indeed dissimulate is likewise unbounded. In "A King" Manganelli explores the ambiguous relationship between humanity, in the person of a king, who has the ability to create language, and animals, who have no language, and who cannot name but can only be named. Initially the king takes on the characteristics of creatures he considers to be linked unequivocally to kingliness, all of whom are subject to his power, which eventually proves not to be limitless after all.

The second text is likewise a hallucinatory monologue, but with a speaker more akin to Prince Hamlet than a king. "Simulations" displays a strong narrative impulse, with the main player dazzlingly adept at metamorphosis and disguise. The protagonist here resembles the creative artist as sovereign, exploring themes developed in other works by Manganelli, particularly the fraught, often violent relationship between mother and son — again a reflection of *Hamlet*. "Simulations" develops in two ways, either by expanding the scope of a particular element, or by changing locations and introducing different scenarios. The self of the narrator is elusive and fragile, and his relationships with others, even their existence, is precarious. The section that deals with the onset of war is more sustained. Here the ruler divides in two to become both the legitimate sovereign and his enemy, the sovereign's other, a revolutionary. The narrative element of Manganelli's style, which several of his fellow members of the Italian neo-avant-garde criticised as reactionary, is here fully developed, but with a disregard for limitations of space, time or character: Calvino particularly admired this aspect of Manganelli's skill. The piece advances with extreme rapidity, shifting from one scene to another like rapid cutting in a film. The world it depicts is dark and cruel, sometimes recalling adventure fiction from the 19th century but exploiting its literary antecedents only to surpass them, given that the ability to simulate is unlimited. "Simulations" ends with the image of an "imperfect child", an echo of the close to "A King", and in both cases the text avoids obvious pathos while simultaneously revealing the poignancy inherent in a literature that aspires to infinite freedom but is nevertheless circumscribed by language.

The central, shorter pieces are on a different scale and show a more tentative approach to narrative development; they become almost entirely cerebral. No longer are we being addressed directly; we eavesdrop on the internal conversations of those who have died but who continue to create their fictions, as in "Ignominy", or those whose existence is haunted by the idea of suicide, as in "A Few Hypotheses Concerning My Previous Reincarnations". The recovery of the past through memory is a traditional literary trope, but in this text Manganelli undermines it by making permeable the boundaries between life and death. Here memory carries the central character into the past before his birth, to uncover the four different incarnations he has undergone, accompanied by suicide, which is envisaged as a companion or guide.

The "plot" in this text is the most complex in the book, and the reader may benefit from a summary. The narrator's exploration develops by his putting forward hypotheses to explain the significance of his recollected suicide, which signifies to him a problem that needs to be solved. As his enquiry proceeds, the narrator, who like everyone else carries within himself a "plan" for his own death, finds himself in a dialogue with another, a "deity", and realises that his suicide has a theological aspect. He concludes that in the first of his reincarnations he was a priest who killed himself, driven by a hatred which originated in yet another previous existence. He now discovers within his memory an existence when he was a man who killed someone in a crime of passion, and who may have been publicly executed (an idea which he later rejects). The more the narrator attempts to understand his former existences the more complex those former lives become, particularly when the boundaries between separate reincarnations begin to break down. Each reincarnation is marked by a different kind of hatred, and all his efforts to resolve the problems presented by these manifestations of hatred fail.

His reincarnation as a priest, when he desired a woman who wished to be killed, appears to carry the greatest significance, for here he can address the theological aspect of suicide; but this priestly role is still only one of his reincarnations and others may yet await his discovery.

In "Ignominy" the protagonist seems to be already dead, and since he is without dimensions he is compared to a thread striving to pass through the eye of a needle. The narrator has no idea how or why he died and meditates on the different ways in which he could have met his death, a nondescript death possibly, or perhaps murder, even self-murder. But these deaths are without honour, compared to taking on the role of an assassin. In this text, the shortest in the book, the writer strips away incident, character and movement, and replaces them with a void and an anonymous narrator who blindly seeks to achieve an impossible task. It is a remarkably austere text in comparison to the others.

"An Impossible Love" consists of an exchange of letters, delivered by a "verbal catapult", between Hamlet, the hero of Shakespeare's 17th-century tragedy, and the Princess of Clèves, the eponymous heroine of the later, but also 17th-century French novel. Manganelli assumes some prior knowledge from the reader about these texts, while not hesitating to alter aspects of them in his own narrative.

Hamlet, first performed around 1600 and first published in 1603, is the revenge tragedy *par excellence*. Hamlet's father has been murdered by Claudius who then claims the throne and marries Hamlet's mother. Young Hamlet, who has a claim to that throne, meets his father's ghost, who tells him of Claudius's crime and urges him to take revenge. The duty imposed on Hamlet by his deceased father is complicated by doubts over the validity of the ghost, and the requirement that in pursuit of that revenge Hamlet should not plot against his mother nor sacrifice his own nobility. The courtier Polonius forbids his daughter Ophelia to continue her relationship with Hamlet, and the distress brought about by this estrangement and the death of her father, accidentally killed by Hamlet, leads her to lose her mind and eventually drown herself. For much of the play Hamlet assumes "an antic disposition", in effect playing the fool in Claudius's court, with a constant use of wit and word-play disguising the fact that he is intent on vengeance. Hamlet shares this strategy with his friends, particularly his close companion at the University of Wittenberg, Horatio. At the close of the play, Hamlet impulsively kills Claudius, but dies himself, from a cut from the rapier poisoned by the king. Manganelli initially adopts the main elements of Shakespeare's tragedy, but attributes the construction of the verbal catapult to Marcellus, a soldier, rather than to his scholar friend, Horatio, to alert us to the fact that this is his own *Hamlet*.

The Princess of Clèves was first published anonymously in 1678, and although there is some dispute over the authorship it is generally agreed that it was written by Madame de La Fayette.[5] Its significance derives both from the fact that its author was a woman and from its being perhaps the earliest example of a psychological novel. Both *Hamlet* and *The Princess of Clèves* are set in Renaissance courts beset with intrigue and deception, but in the latter these intrigues concern the courtiers' numerous love affairs rather than any political manœuvring. Guided by the moral precepts of her mother, the princess marries the Prince of Clèves, even though she does not love him, as he is well aware. Her exceptional beauty attracts the Duke (or sometimes the Count, Manganelli uses both) of Nemours, notorious at court for his numerous liaisons. He falls in love with the princess and spurns his mistresses because of the devotion he feels for her. She in turn falls deeply in love with Nemours; however, the burden of denying that love and suppressing any open display of it oppresses her so greatly that eventually she confesses to her husband that she is in love with a member of the court, and Nemours overhears this conversation. Her husband, who has never ceased to love her, is devastated and presses her for the name of her lover, but she refuses to say. Eventually he discovers it is Nemours and wrongly believes that his wife has been unfaithful; the anguish of this brings about his death. The princess now finds herself free to marry, yet rejects Nemours, blaming him but also herself for her husband's death. She withdraws from society, to the Chateau at Coulommiers (Colombelles in the text here), and spends part of the year in a convent — the death of the Prince of Clèves has turned her mind towards "thinking of nothing but the life hereafter." Her husband is not the only character to die in the course of the novel since her mother also dies, as does the Duke of Guise, a former suitor of hers, and the king too, after being wounded in a tournament.

At first glance, the form of "An Impossible Love" resembles an epistolary novel from the 18th century,[6] but Manganelli plays upon the conflict between the genres of novel and drama so that sometimes we are listening to their letters, and at other times reading them. As this conversation proceeds other characters intervene, the most significant being Ophelia and the ghost. Hamlet, provoked by the sight of his father's spectre, writes to the princess in order to welcome and challenge death, and, in an act of defiance, to break through into another kind of existence, "a world beyond the script". The princess is also concerned with mortality, though hers is a world without phantoms; her "disobedience" has been the denial of her love for the Duke of Nemours. Together, these distinctive characters, acknowledging the decadence and decay all around them, face the oncoming end of their worlds. The ghost of Hamlet's father takes on a significant role in which he appears to converse with phantoms from other worlds, perhaps from the future, and has an ambiguous relation with death that involves an inversion of the vampire myth. The ghost transports himself into the princess's domain of Colombelles by way of the "verbal catapult" because, after all, he is nothing but words. Hamlet employs the same resource to join the princess, and the catapult also functions as a sort of time machine which transports Hamlet into a "region of darkness" where he will remain forever listening to "the ticking of infinite clocks", deprived of death now that he has exited the stage of the Globe Theatre ("the wooden O"), where he enacted himself in a performance that always ended with his death.

The final text, "Disquisition on the Difficulty of Communicating with the Dead", takes as its model a learned treatise within which Manganelli's fantastical imagination is both liberated yet tightly controlled. It was this text which Calvino immediately recognised as a modern classic, describing its author in his foreword "as the most trustworthy compiler of the hallucinations and deliriums of the public and private ego in this our antechamber of Hades." If "An Impossible Love" is a pastiche of the 18th-century epistolary novel, "Disquisition" harks back to the 17th-century world of Burton's *Anatomy of Melancholy* with its eccentric, scholarly narrator who can only write, in his "execrably impoverished style... by dipping the feeble quill of my invention into the blackest of midnight inks." Through a series of "grotesque and desperate explorations" by "scholars of mortality", to discover the nature of the dead, to attempt to trace their location in the world or the universe, to discover what language they might speak or understand, or what etiquette to employ when seeking to initiate a dialogue with them, Manganelli creates a virtuosic display of increasingly absurd and complex solutions to the impossible questions he has set himself.

What is it like to be one of Manganelli's "impossible readers"? To read an author like this inevitably challenges our idea of what fiction should be. In Manganelli's world, as we would expect, the familiar is rendered unfamiliar, but his originality lies in the extremity of that strangeness: paradoxes replace assertion, categorical boundaries are treated as non-existent or something to be ignored at will; being alive and dead can be experienced simultaneously; ghosts exhibit all the foibles of living personalities; gods are piled upon gods in worlds falling into oblivion; cities are sacked and so are the landmarks of European literature. All is subject to but one subordination: the necessities of language itself.

Some of the ideas expressed in "Literature as Deception" may lead one to believe that Manganelli risked creating texts that are unstructured, even nonsensical, but this is far from the case. Despite Manganelli's perpetual contest with language and his bizarre conceptions, the texts, while retaining a sense of spontaneity and improvisation, also display all the control necessary to produce the "dynamic ambiguity" he claims for them. Blanchot considered literature to be "language turning into ambiguity";[7] Manganelli exploits this ambiguity almost to excess. In a review of Calvino's *Six Memos for the Next Millennium* Manganelli made the distinction between "limpidity" and "clarity": the former presents us with texts that are one-dimensional and transparent, resistant to any attempt to penetrate below the surface; "clarity" on the other hand creates writing that exists in many dimensions, allowing the reader "to see precisely what lies beyond the text, whether near it, around it, or behind it",[8] thus creating "a text of greater dimensions, of infinite dimensions, that are deceptive, hallucinatory and enigmatic." This is what it is like to read Manganelli.

NOTES

1. Edgar Allan Poe, *I Racconti (1831-49)*, Einaudi, Turin, 1990.

2. The group first met in 1963 and broke up six years later.

3. A detailed account of Manganelli's relationship with Gruppo 63 can be found in Mussgnug, pp.10-28 (see note following).

4. Florian Mussgnug, *The Eloquence of Ghosts*, Peter Lang, Bern, 2010.

5. Madame de La Fayette, *The Princesse de Clèves*, trans. Terence Cave, Oxford University Press, 1999.

6. Manganelli wrote a short study of the 18th-century English novel: *Il romanzo inglese del Settecento*, Nino Aragno, Turin, 2004.

7. Maurice Blanchot, "Literature and the Right to Death", in *The Station Hill Blanchot Reader*, Station Hill Press, Barrytown, 2000, p.396.

8. Manganelli in Calvino, in *Antologia privata*, Rizzoli, Milan, 1989, p.163.

FOREWORD

Italo Calvino

●

"It seems to me to be beyond question that I am a King. I possess a kingly way of thinking, of contemplating and of imagining, that never ceases to amaze and delight me. I am unable to think of ignoble or ordinary things; everything must be given a name and take its place within a hierarchy, and stride or crawl, but in an emblematic way. I think of eagles, especially in the first light of dawn, in the silence between night and day, in the numbing cold, amidst the flowers' careless sorrow. I think of huge eagles, with their metallic wings and the piercing malevolence of their eyes..."

Manganelli's new book begins with this peremptory opening and then launches into a crescendo of variations on its main theme, the self-aggrandisement of a lucid megalomaniac. The solitude of the insomniac protagonist, who tosses and turns in his sheets as though they were the blank pages of a book, conjures up a series of heraldic animals, symptoms of his dark euphoria. The theatre on which Manganelli once again raises the curtain for his verbal spectacle is the space of the mind: it is populated by ghosts which all converge on the supreme allegory, death, the most carnivalesque and sumptuous object in the scenic backdrop inside our head. But in place of the self-destructive violence of his *Hilarotragoedia*, with its desire for the final descent, and instead of the architecture that raised up monumental gates and horizontal beams on top of a frozen pinhead in *Nuovo commento*, here we find the energetic tension of a *raptus*, someone snatched up and hovering on wings in the grandiose skies of simulation, swooping low over the vortices of absence. An inexhaustible obsession for deduction leads to labyrinthine perspectives crowded with a proliferation of mythical figures, of multitudes of gods or of the dead: gods in clusters, gods in tangles, dough to make gods with; as for the limitless population of the dead, they swarm around the screw threads of a big, rusty bolt, their secret receptacle and their microscopic Avernus, or they are covered in flour and cooked in an underworld focaccia. In the six chapters of this profoundly unified book — although it is varied to the point of including an exchange of letters between Hamlet and the Princess of Clèves, and the already classic "Disquisition on the Difficulty of Communicating with the Dead" — our author offers no shortage of surprises, innovations in tone and invention, which are as striking as those areas where he is obstinately faithful to himself. The mystification works with the naturalness of a living organism, thanks to a particular mechanism whose secret is fought over by Manganelli the writer in a duel with Manganelli the theoriser of "Literature as Deception". This erudite acrobat who twirls about on the trapeze of rhetoric above the timeless void of meaning may one day be recognised as the most trustworthy compiler of the hallucinations and deliriums of the public and private ego in this our antechamber of Hades.

ITERATURE AS
DECEPTION

uring a discussion some time ago, one of those present claimed that, "As long as there's a single child somewhere in the world dying of hunger, the writing of literature is immoral." One of the others commented, "Well, that's always been the case."

Let us suppose that the wisdom of our rulers, the systematic anger of the ruled and the charitable collaboration of wind and rain allow the announcement, a few generations hence, that: "From today, Monday, no child will ever again die of hunger." Would some sincere and rational thinker not immediately turn up to remind us about suicides, premature deaths and crimes of passion and alcoholism? Isn't this special animosity which literature has always attracted rather a sign that humanity — and above all those one might describe as humanists — has always suspected it of being an immoral activity? And isn't it this very immorality, this quasi-human characteristic which is intrinsic to literature both as an object and an activity, that makes it unbearable to the humanity which is also its host?

There are certain animals with abundant fur, whose pointed faces and abstract buttocks are emblazoned with a whole dictionary of precise images. Their body is unified and nurtured by a synthesis of signs, a network of bold isoglosses, garish and silent, which create a discourse from these random elements that is both artificial and inspired. An absurd and authoritative nobility decorates this alien body as it comports itself, at once oblivious to the colours it displays and to the fierce and aggressive escutcheon that marks its status. In the same way humanity carries around with it a useless and prestigious standard, a cloak and shroud that does not suit its body: an ill-fitting yet magnificent sheath. Just as the mandrill is unable to dull the rhetoric of its multi-coloured arse, so humanity cannot slough off — delightful curse — this pliant fleece of words.

Perhaps it is true, literature is immoral, and it is immoral to devote any time to it. It would be no less intolerable if it simply took no notice of mankind's anguish and refused to tend his ancient wounds; instead, insolently and with painstaking patience, it hunts them down, searching for them in order to bring about anxieties, illness and death: with passionate indifference, with bitter fury and stubborn cynicism it selects them, juxtaposes them, dissects them, manipulates them and cuts them open once again. A purulent wound blooms into a metaphor, a massacre becomes nothing more than a hyperbole and madness the ability to distort language beyond repair, revealing its movement, gestures and unforeseeable outcomes. Suffering is nothing more than a means for language to organise itself: it is how it functions.

Self-evidently, literature is cynical. There is no lechery it does not embrace, no ignoble sentiment, hatred, anger or sadism in which it does not delight, no tragedy that does not coolly excite it as it seeks to comprehend the careful, malicious intelligence that governs it. Consider, by way of contrast, how tentatively and with what imaginative sarcasm it handles the symptoms of decency.

The rage of the respectable against literature is well attested. For centuries it has been accused of fraud, corruption and impiety. Of being both purposeless and poisonous. Defiling and perverse, it nevertheless enchants and distresses. Numinous and changeable, it does not hesitate to employ some of the gods as ornaments for its fairy tales. But through that exquisite irony which defines its destiny, literature alone knows how to properly celebrate the grandeur and glory of that god which it degrades and ennobles as a character, a hypotyposis or a hyperbole. The terrible hurler of thunderbolts, having entered the fragile net of rhetoric, ceases to exist completely, and is transformed into an invention, a game or a deception.

Being corrupt, literature knows how to feign piety: gloriously deformed, it enforces the sadistic coherence of syntax; unreal, it offers us falsehoods and endless magical epiphanies. Being devoid of emotions, it makes use of all of them. Its coherence is born out of its lack of sincerity. Having cast out its soul it finds its own destiny.

Everyone may approach it, and none will leave unharmed. Rather: no one is immune. There is no saint so removed from civilisation that he does not harbour within himself the wasting syphilis of literature. *Ciceronianus sum.*[1] Hence the primeval love and anger aroused by this admirable and unclean thing, this ferocious, this docile yet ominously omnivorous creature.

Some among those all too-numerous great writers contemplated eliminating literature altogether. A delightful struggle with their own entrails. Others, liberals and humanists, nowadays want to reform it, just as they did in the past. Periodically someone dreams of a definitive Good Shepherd, and a kingdom where learned gentlemen with nasal voices will prepare literature for noble missions. Or, with a lawyer's passion or a sophist's cunning, they reveal that after all literature already works towards improving humanity's lot, and that it is both enlightening and useful. They scrape the dirt off the epidermis of metaphor until the Spirit of the Times is revealed, along with a slimy residue, almost white in colour: this is the *Weltanschauung.* However, being a seductress by vocation, literature rejects the role of virtuous wife, or honest and unsophisticated companion. Vainly they try to persuade her to become the teacher of healthy heterosexual sons, an industrious and elegant consort. But this loose woman will turn into a dockside prostitute or a truck drivers' whore. In opposition to our mortality she sets her predilection for death — that invariable figure of speech.

It is a never-ending scandal. And this is why it is so difficult to become one of her adherents. The world tempts us, and wants us to be gentlemen. We can define literature as an *adynaton,* something impossible which transforms absolutely everything into a figure of speech. It is indifferent to humanity and maintains contact with it only to the extent that human beings cease to be human. The moment literature manages to persuade any one of them, even implicitly, that suffering, injustice and horror are nothing more than a *Gradus ad Parnassum,*[2] a device for revealing imperfectible syntax, then that person is possessed: he will be led into unforgivable sin, it makes him an adulterer, a murderer and a cheat, and he finds himself pleased to be so. It crowns him a deserter.

There can be no literature without desertion, disobedience, indifference and wholesale rejection of the soul. But desertion from what? From every communal obligation, from every approval of one's own or others' sense of loyalty, every social commandment. In the first place, the writer chooses to be useless; how often that ancient insult of practical men is thrown in his face: "buffoon". Well so be it: the writer *is* a buffoon. He is the *fool:* that approximately human being who turns impiety, mockery and indifference into something very close to homicidal power. The buffoon has no place in history; he is a joke, a mistake.

Fundamentally asocial, the deserter must work out strategies of escape according to the coercive structures of his time. He detests discipline and a clear conscience, and the collusion of the one with the other is fatal to him. Wherever that laughable *middle-aged* being, Man, triumphs, he must protect himself, deceive and flee. Each day, with a precise and tragic gesture, he must cleanse himself of the euphoric myths of a clear conscience: collective wisdom, progress and justice. With a restless and cowardly sidelong glance, he searches tirelessly for signs of violence: mineral hieroglyphs on a partially human hand, the secretions growing over someone's mouth or the geometrical wounds of decomposition; he is on the side of death, of crooked justice, perfectible with difficulty, and refined paradox — an ironic place at which he arrives only when his journey ends. For his home he chooses subterranean, unsurfaced passageways. He needs a particular kind of liberty, which is different for each author; not a "liberal" liberty, however, for in fact no liberal would tolerate its subversiveness or its blasphemy. Sentimental liberty, with its flavour of honest, consummated collaboration, suffocates him. He can survive in any kind of atmosphere, so long as it is polluted. Where the shadows of optimism prevail he is a stowaway, who, with priestly caution, carries about his person a ciborium of poison. A natural anarchist, he is always in touch with those passageways of the lower depths, packed with heavy drapes and sudden groans, those labyrinths where the virtuous gaze of the humanist does not dare to venture.

Literature, being anarchic, is therefore utopian, and so dissolves and coagulates endlessly. As is proper for utopias, it is childish, annoying and disconcerting.

Writing literature is not a social act. It can find a public, however, despite being literature, but that public is no more than its temporary destination. Literature is created for readers who are indeterminate, about to be born, destined not to be born, already born or already dead; even for impossible readers. Frequently, as with the writings of the insane, it presumes the absence of readers. In consequence, the writer struggles to keep up with events; as in old comedy films he laughs and cries out of turn. His actions seem clumsy yet are secretly precise. His communication with his contemporaries is extremely flawed. He is a lightning flash that comes too late; his arguments are unintelligible to many, even to himself.

He alludes to events that occurred over two centuries or which are yet to happen three generations ago.

The writing of literature is an act of perverse humility. Those who produce literary objects engage with a situation of linguistic provocation. Ensnared, saturated and immersed in a web of verbal trajectories, spurred on by signals, formulas, entreaties and pure sounds eager for collocation, dazzled and chafed by whirlwinds, by wandering trails of words — both voyeur and master of ceremonies, the writer is called to bear witness to the language which contends with him, which has chosen him and which is the only place where it is tolerable for him to exist; the only condition which is stable and real, although actually it is unreal and impermanent; a unique existence then, wherein the writer recognises that he himself is nothing more than a strategy of language, his own invention, perhaps his own ectoplasmic genitalia.

Wrapped up in its convolutions, trapped within the sphere of his language, the writer is neither a contemporary to events, which are unable to conform to a chronology compatible with his biography, nor even to those of other writers with whom he co-exists, except when they too are engaged with the very same language: a situation that is metaphysical rather than historical. It also happens that, through the coercive demands of language, and the acute instability and natural infidelity of the worldly, the writer lives in a state of discontinuous contemporaneity with himself. Thus neither historical events nor the safeguards of literary narrative give us access to literature, but only the act of precisely shaping the language within which literature finds its structure.

Like a witness to a crime, the writer "doesn't know anything": but his way of not knowing is highly specific. He completely ignores the meaning of the language in which he is engaged, and this is the source of his power: his ability to experience it as a pastiche, as an accumulation of impossibilities, falsehoods, hoaxes, illusions, games and rituals. Yet he is also someone who works hard with a hostile and stubborn material. From language which is explicit and fallacious, fluid and combative, he has to construct an object whose compact, solid perfection encloses a dynamic ambiguity. He does not work according to inspiration or imagination, but in obedience to language; he tries to carry out what that barbarous, impetuously oracular god requires. His devotion is fanatical and inadequate. During the production of the verbal object, the condition of learned ignorance is binding. He knows how to create perfectly only that which he does not understand. The object born out of the complicity between his ignorance and his knowledge is totally inaccessible to him. He knows that it is a contrivance, constructed according to the unique and inescapable rules by which such devices are made; but at the same time he does not know what agency will launch this inexhaustible explosive nor the nature and extent of the attacks that will be made; the only secret and detestable hope that consoles him is that, in time, he will end up offending *everyone*. Thus, the author does not, must not, know his own work, not even what others see in it. Furthermore, he has the dim sensation that this ambiguous entity which he has brought into the light with the physical ingenuity and heroic incomprehension common to all mothers, will be violated by every desire to understand what he wants to convey. And although he knows that the work has been condemned to this type of abuse right from the start, the thought of being asked to explain "What is it you want to say?" fills him with complete horror. A natural instinct will lead him always to refuse, or really not to understand what others wish "to understand". The literary object is obscure, dense, corpulent, one might say, opaque and packed with chance complexities; it changes its lines of fracture constantly, and is a silent web of resounding words. Totally ambiguous, able to move in every direction, it is inexhaustible and unreasonable. The literary word is infinitely plausible: its ambiguity makes it imperishable. It projects around itself a halo of meanings; it wishes to say everything and consequently says nothing. Its fragile and incorruptible flesh conceals no tumour of *Weltanschauung.*

(A paragraph of peripheral irascibility: this crude, lucid "not-knowing" leads one to deduce that such a writer will not find himself admitted to the union of miscellaneous intellectuals. And he is all the more abused when, for the sake of his social and historical prestige, he wishes to be included in that laughable fifth state. Better to call him a "buffoon". Obviously the quite repulsive figure of the intellectual is a humanist invention, which today represents only a *genteel* rebellion.)

The literary work is an artifice, an artificial creation with an uncertain and ironically fatal destination. Its artifice encompasses, *ad infinitum,* other artifices; a metallically assembled proposition hides a buzzing metaphor; dissecting it, we will set at liberty strong, exact words, a union of limpid phonemes. In the body of the proposition, the words organise themselves with a chaotic rigour, like ceremonial dancers lost in thought: they strive for the hypallage that will locate them at the reciprocal aphelion, the chiasmus that situates them in mirror-like immobility; they align themselves with the enunciated procession of anaphora, and brave the vertigo of oxymorons, or the compliant disobedience of the anacoluthon; tmesis imitates an attack of schizophrenia, homoeoteleuton is pure echolalia. Viewed from outside, the articulation of rhetoric resembles a lunatic assemblage. The paranoid's peroration is integrated into a manic-depressive monologue. The objective of such rhetorical fictions is always to attain an irreducible ambiguity. The writer's fate is to work with ever greater knowledge of a text which is increasingly unrelated to sense. Dispassionate exorcisms unleash a passionate dynamic of linguistic invention.

Images, words, the various structures of the literary object are all restricted to movements which have the rigour and arbitrariness of ritual; and it is precisely in ritual that literature reaches the summit of mystifying revelation. Because they are dead, all the gods and all the demons belong to literature; and it is literature itself that has killed them. At the same time literature derives its power from them, along with its indifference and its ability to inspire miracles. Literature organises itself as a pseudo-theology, in which a whole universe is celebrated, both its end and its beginning, with its rites and its hierarchies, its immortal and mortal beings: everything is precise, and everything is a lie.

And it is here that the fantastic provocation of literature, with its heroic and mythological bad faith, is gathered together and unified. With propositions that are "devoid of sense" and "unverifiable" affirmations, it invents universes and simulates inexhaustible ceremonies. It possesses, and manages nothingness, which it organises according to a catalogue of designs, signs and models. It provokes us and challenges us, offering us the skin of an illusory, heraldic wild animal, a complex device, a die, a relic and the incidental irony of a coat of arms.

(1967)

NOTES

1. "I am Ciceronian." A reference to Christianity's debt to Cicero's famously powerful rhetoric, from Petrarch, *De Ignorantia*, book 4, alluding to St. Jerome, Epistle 22.

2. Literally "Steps towards Parnassus", but the *Gradus* was also a huge Latin thesaurus used by Latin scholars between the 17th and early 20th centuries.

O THOSE GODS
BEYOND

A KING

It seems to me to be beyond question that I am a King. I possess a kingly way of thinking, of contemplating and imagining, that never ceases to amaze and delight me. I am unable to think of ignoble or ordinary things; everything must be given a name and take its place within a hierarchy, and stride or crawl, but in an emblematic way. I think of eagles, especially in the first light of dawn, in the silence between night and day, in the numbing cold, amidst the flowers' careless sorrow. I think of huge eagles, with their metallic wings and the piercing malevolence of their eyes. A murderous beak, despotic and unswayed by passion. And all about my kin, the eagle, a limitless space extends; he is fierce too, but if he can be considered simply as geometry and nothing else, then I am only a wound with wings, a beak-shaped gash in the sky, the beak's signature on the vault of the heavens. Perhaps some will regard this image as tiresomely baroque; well then, he is no king, and consequently I will give no further explanation. I do not know if the eagle, in search of respite, can rest upon the clouds, or if the vast span of his wings is enough to sustain his equilibrium even in sleep; but the eagle I am thinking of scorns the branches of trees, and the earth is simply the topography where his prey roams. All the animals that flee or fly close to the ground, that climb up into the trees, that make their hiding places among roots or live in the undergrowth, or that disguise themselves in the autumn or summer, all of these are his subjects and if they attempt to escape his claws they are nothing more to him than rebellious subjects and so deserve death twice over. His eye creates a continual rapid blueprint of the world, and no creature is so small that it can withdraw from his inventory of death. However, his eye has no commerce with his subjects, except in that moment when he kills them. And this is the moment too when the animal, badly mauled but still half alive and hanging from the claws of its divine destroyer, experiences the vertiginous verticality of flight, which is completely alien to it, and which for all its brief and departing life it has both feared and longed for.

The eagle's fearful, silent exhilaration gives me a joy that would be a waste of my time to try to explain; and perhaps it is not an absolute joy, since I often wake from this delight, or rather I start up suddenly with my eyes full of tears. Then, with the kingly gaze that he and I know of old, we part from one another, and one after the other plunge into space, then hurtle along parallel to the ground, fated to meet again at the next twilight.

I stir in my great empty bed, shift the pillows, and let a new image worthy of me rise up in my mind. I consider the lion. His powerful scent fills the room, spills out over the countryside; the whole world, the cosmos, smells of urine, grass and butchered meat. (Notice how these creatures enjoy a personal pronoun which utterly fails to match their dimensions, and yet I can tolerate such a monologue with myself conducted with the austerity of human pronouns by ensuring that they are not diminished by such designations.) The lion takes on, like a new fabric, a colour he has skimmed from the centre of the sun. The earth he crosses is scorched, as if raked by claws over and again; his scent slowly spells out death to all the different animals, nameless and swift. Such is the cunning of the lion: that he, a constellation of flesh and a comet of claws, feigns to exist on the same level as the creatures he kills. I see the lion's colour as what defines him, rather than his ferocity, which is already a part of the eagle's universal behaviour. The lion clothes himself in woodland, in autumn sun, flame, gorse and pus: he preserves his hunger intact, and the diversion created by his hunger. All this makes him worthy of my consideration. Apart from his colour, I have spoken of his scent; but this smell is not something independent, it accompanies his roar. According to the direction of the wind, the lion's flesh sends out a double message, harsh and unsettling — the scent that contaminates the world with lordly death, and the roar that calls out a warning of it. The animals flee as one, but this male lion does not conceal himself, being fully aware that he is known for being the animal who will eat them. In fact, it is only the creature he devours that is given a name; the others, nameless and unholy, are simply signs in the air, non-existent. His gaping jaws baptise the creature that is devoured, a way of satisfying his hunger that is catastrophic. I think it may be possible, in my kingliness, to create a lion with apocalyptic jaws, a lion-galaxy who, with his urine, scent and his roar, would terrify and baptise the whole world, with hunger and jaws vast enough to maim and devour it. I curl the fingers of my hand and watch them follow the wishes of my claws. I push aside a pillow and bring to mind my regal colleague, the serpent.

The chill that traverses my brain from one side to the other reminds me acutely that I am definitely one with him; for this one's coldness is as dear to me as the eagle's beak or the lion's colour. The serpent is a length of silent, flexible ice; his pliant nature is to be as long as the world, and since the world is round, to reach around it until he can bite his own tail, and thus bind the whole of it within his circle. I travel along the serpent's scales, each step the length of a mountain chain, but the serpent ever renews itself; one day I delight in his rose-coloured scales, exorbitant and elegant, the sensuousness of his narrow, fleshy body and his languid and lethargic sexual allusiveness; on another day his scales are tattooed on both sides with traces of writing, the different scripts all scrambled altogether and with texts overlapping, so that the journey leads to wisdom and becomes hermetic, as if travelling a ruined Hellenistic road past a series of illuminating and repellent relics. On another day I revel in the fineness of his shadowy links, this night that girdles the planet like a thread; on yet another day he sparkles with gold, he is a diadem, a bracelet, a necklace that makes the world his courtier, ready to sell itself for a poisonous jewel that is merely a bauble. He kills by penetration, not by crushing or mauling, and injects into the dying creature that substance which in him is most himself, which brings no harm to himself, and is indeed crowned with a halo. First he lures his prey, then entraps it, encircles it; next he enters it as a liquid, a deadly semen. For a moment the poisoned creature takes on the nature of the serpent; they share the same mortal presence and the dying creature experiences an irrefutable moment of congress during which it grasps its inability to be a part of the serpent-king except as something dead, in other words as food. They say that the snake radiates sleep, but when I study him within myself I would say rather that he gives off a slow and awkward ecstasy, the power of his meditating will, which is so intense and static that it cannot be reconciled with the trivialities of existence. He is a creature of silence, except in that moment of assignation with the dead animal, and is perfectly camouflaged. Sometimes, if I did not know him so intimately, I would not know how to track him down again, and would suspect he was everywhere, just as mortals do. His silence has a remarkable nobility, so that his prey, being fully aware that he and silence are one and the same thing — a silence capable of co-existing with all the sounds of life yet which still remains absolute — his prey, as I was saying, namely those creatures not yet overcome by his gaze or made into a momentary blood-relative by the sharing of poison, everywhere fear him, and in this way he convinces them of his ubiquity. We should note that he swallows his prey whole, once it has been seduced and overcome, and transforms it into himself;

consequently, if I could imagine a serpent of sufficient grandeur, the fate of the universe would be to unravel slowly in his endless gut. Although he resembles a thread, the serpent has no specific shape; he can coil himself up, he can make himself resemble a stream of water, even water itself, or he can become a straight line along the whole length of his body, or cover the world with an infinity of coils; he is as changeable as a constellation and can replicate all geometrical forms, and even sketch out the outlines of different animals and famous men; he is his own pencil. He is thus the silent creator of himself as jewel, bracelet or profile, and can devise highly original silhouettes. He seduces, falls silent, changes; but he conforms to his being as a line and, accordingly, has no thickness: he represents nothing, this wise, insinuating poisoner. He differs from the eagle in having no subjects; his fame is a thing of silence, but he decorates the world and destroys it. A straight and kingly line.

Sometimes the immensity, the sheer span of my thought causes these constellations of feathers, flesh or a straight line to occupy the same space, albeit without any one gaining ascendancy over the others, by virtue of the different dimensions, or ideal royal palaces which they inhabit. So I listen to the silence in my brain and pose questions. Does the eagle, that solitary denizen of the skies, that voracious reader, know that the serpent is not one of his subjects? Does the lion know that he cannot placate his hunger with this fistful, this acre of wind-blown feathers? Does the serpent know that he can neither embellish nor destroy the lion's scent? I ask myself if they even see one another, whether they are aware of their existence within me. Perhaps the special silence that sustains these beasts is merely the sign of a decision proper to each of them, *not* to know each other — which is not the same as being unaware of the others' existence — because each one cannot be undone by the others, and all three incorporate a complete kingliness. However, when I think of the eagle, the lion and the serpent all together I experience a kind of desperate exhaustion, as if I were the object of a coronation being carried out simultaneously in different places, relating to different peoples, while different anthems in counterpoint overlap and intertwine with one another. So, I am King.

Rising from my regal bed, pushing aside the reams of sheets and yielding to the call of the sun, as tawny as the lion, my mind turns to the smaller animals: I open the palm of my hand and imagine a frog there, and we look at one another, questioningly, and I recall that once there were frogs that could transform themselves into princesses, which is a youthful, immature form of regality; there were toad princes too, but could not this frog, having emerged from my brain, enclose within himself some aspects of kingliness? In my mind I place a tiny golden crown on the frog's small head; it suits him. Is there such a thing as a miniature kingliness, a thing of water and croaks, something slippery and skittish that a hand might contain? I gaze tenderly on this slight, green prince, and suggest he jumps. He returns my gaze, cautiously and diffidently. His soft body is a tender bladder of water; I do not kiss him, and so his kingliness — about which I now have my suspicions — is left alone, untouched. I place him in the river where I catch a silver fish. I hold him in a part of my brain that is full of water, in a glass vase of sea-thoughts; I scrutinise his small silver soul, all pale and quivering; the eloquence of his round mouth raises a smile when he feigns to lecture or compose some highly wrought entreaty; oh, this one is a courtier! and out of kindness I restore him to his native waters. And this butterfly, is this not a king, a queen or a king's concubine? A harlot of air and flowers passes before my eyes; as a king I allow myself impure thoughts. I push aside the shameless provocation of these fleeing colours, and punish myself with grubs, worms and spiders; these cannot be kingly, but misshapen and nocturnal as they are, they show signs of having lived in the vicinity of kingliness, a kingliness I could not possibly describe as lion, eagle or snake. I let myself creep along in the intricate form of a snail, all silver slime and patience. Perhaps the day will come when he will be appointed lord chamberlain. A green tortoise contemplates a century-long journey. I have no doubts over the kingliness of the tortoise, but he has no subjects, for he himself is the world's subject, if it be true that the whole cosmos is balanced on his powerful, impenetrable carapace. His ponderousness gives his gait a stately manner, a progress such as only intensely kingly creatures dare to undertake; otherwise he is demonstrably unaware of his own kingliness, is wanting in arrogance, and seems to display a complete lack of regal awareness.

Briefly I consider other possible courtiers: beings touched with a kingliness that is no more than an expression of their disdain, ludicrous, obsequious creatures, paid killers, purveyors of momentary levity, jesters, creatures with agile limbs and quick tongues — chameleons, crickets, gnats, chaffinches, thrushes, shellfish. I wonder about the ridiculous chicken but then reject it, postpone a conversation with the cat with a reciprocated nod of the head (we go back a long way), I examine the pack of hounds and admire the upturned angelic nature of the bat. The opossum, antipodean Polonius, will you be my counsellor, or my hired killer, or even my destroyer? I laugh and start to dress.

My momentary laughter sounds throughout the royal palace; all metals vibrate in response to it, however subdued it is; for copper and bronze love me, tin and pewter obey me, and iron and steel serve me gladly.

The first of these metals are vocal, choral and melodic; they laugh along with my laugh, sometimes rather coarsely, for it is difficult to maintain devotion within the limitations of the high style of courtliness; the dark voices of the other metals attempt to cleanse the air, so that my laughter can shine more brightly without contamination, neither veiled in dust nor obscured by clouds or inimical distances;

these metals do not understand laughter, though they bow down before it, knowing that, even more than I am, it is their master, and that it is this that justifies their being; they are afraid to let its aggressive and subdued beginnings escape; and from this comes a certain baseness, a wary abjection in their engagement; but can there be kingliness without the ignoble being present too? So I do not insult them, nor show contempt, for base metals always derive from me and I alone understand them. The more precious metals neither love nor serve my mirth, but are proud of it, and certainly consider it a special proof of my bravery, as it quite clearly is, although they never know why I laugh, nor what form my laugh may take. Even though they do not understand it, they are deeply moved, as if it were a major trial of faith or something that brings them honour and glorifies them. They laugh in their gladness, in their pride at participating in my laughter; they sparkle, and I feel sure they are nourished by it. Yet I have never allowed myself a huge obscene horse-laugh, nor indulged in a prolonged and trifling snigger, or some uncouth and disgustingly loud guffaw, nor a feeble hysterical giggle that goes on for ever; actually my laugh is more like a cough, the idea of a laugh, with a quick curl of the lips and a catch in the throat, and what is more it is quite lacking in sarcasm, irony or casual arrogance; indeed, if it were not for iron's simple pride, the perfunctory polish of tin and pewter and the joyful wink of copper, perhaps I would not be aware that I had laughed at all. But now all of my royal palace is briefly shaken, and my laughter is restored to me with daring, with dedication and a temerity that no one comprehends, and I must accept it as a strange gift that issues from me and returns, enriched by the willing collaboration of these courtiers of metal.

My laughter is also strategic; in fact, once it leaves me, it travels across the vast space of my royal palace and surveys it. Such is the extent of my palace that no physical body would be able to cross it, unless it was possessed of incredible dimensions or was able to employ some particularly tortuous and flexible system of time. For this reason I have chosen a means of surveillance that is formless. My swift laugh travels through the interminable corridors like a nimble-winged creature; through endless rooms it passes through triumphal arches, surveys the narrow passageways, attics and cellars; although it is weak, all objects respond to it, the fabrics, carpets, window-glass, tapestries and other ornaments, the chests brimful of kingly vestments; the thrones quiver, so too the crystal of the chandeliers, the halberds in the armoury, the arquebuses and mangonels on the terraces, the pennants fluttering in the wind, the sundial's gnomon and the water in the cistern. Everything that is touched or stroked by the laughter of kingliness replies with its ancient traditional sign of approbation, or at least recognises itself as the legitimate target of this laughter, its possession perhaps, or even its slave. My laugh informs the whole royal palace that I am in my chamber and am exercising my power. And when it returns to me I touch it and stroke it as if it were a messenger bird, acknowledging it as whole, intact, slight and compact.

It is not always this swift bird of laughter that I dispatch to survey my royal palace; if the last thought before I awakened was of a fish from the watery depths, a shark, I might send out a shiver, a powerful movement of disgust; and then I would hear back the awkward and uneasy vibrations of metals that already live in fear of being condemned, either by being excluded from my love, or by the bravery that everywhere accompanies me; or I give out a sigh, a gust that springs from the palm of my hand, a swirling passage of air in pursuit of a butterfly, a cold grassy sigh in the form of a chameleon or an angry sigh like that of a feline. Sometimes I send forth a click of the fingers that bounces crudely and argumentatively from room to room, or a snap of my jaw that intimidates the breeze and distresses the tapestries. This wafting pennant of wind groans sometimes, at other times entreats or quivers and quakes with fear; it is childish and extremely sensitive.

The colour of the air and the mood of the weather changes according to the messenger I appoint to survey my palace. The sweet indulgence of the breeze may give way to sulphurous oppression, or to the cool languor of a sickly snake, or the cloudy and gloomy temperament of the fragmentary and melancholy light that shines from a sunless sky. So it is that not only my palace but everything around it becomes concentrated in its movement like a wheel and yields in obedience to my kingliness. The castle battlements deliberate over my inspector and inform the winds and the stars: whether it was laughter, or a sigh, and of what kind. Everything that surrounds me seeks this news, so as to know how to obey me. So vast is my palace that often the return of my diminutive laugh is delayed, detained by some game perhaps, by the innumerable timepieces, the genial grandfather clocks; or the sighs allow themselves to become entangled in the magniloquent gossip of curtains, or decline to leave the pensive, turbid water of the fountain thick with moss; or they play about the weathervane with the winds, so much more powerful than they are, yet still compliant. Perhaps too the infinite dwelling with its labyrinthine articulation is enough for my laugh to lose track of a journey which has been prolonged out of all proportion. Sometimes my messenger from one day only returns the day afterwards, or I find it close by at the moment when I wake up again, even though I have not explicitly authorised it to intrude into my dreams.

A horse that started off at a wild unbridled gallop through these halls would be a skeleton before it had covered a fifth of its journey; I seem to know that right at the centre of the royal palace sits the shell of a dead tortoise, which was overcome by exhaustion or by the extraordinarily particular nature of its location, the boss of the shield. Perhaps families of bacteria could plan a full exploration of the palace, by establishing an itinerary which they would then pass on from one generation to another. But what would be the point of sending through the palace a life-form which, through a defect of grammar and poverty of vocabulary, had no tales to tell? Might one employ a more cultured and learned bacterium? Perhaps I will try. Any exploration of the royal palace, however, can only ever be a form of demagogy, since this residence was conceived by me, just as I conceived the bloody constellation of the lion. Consequently I know it completely, although I have never explored it, and while I dwell here, it also dwells in me, so that I am both smaller and larger than it, at one and the same time.

My palace is, essentially, circular. I say "essentially" as I maintain that this shape, on the basis of its complete kingliness, may yet be in some way ordinary, or that it at least parades a kingliness that is closed in on itself, either from fear of external violence, or out of love for its own everlasting monologue. Thus do I delight in imagining the palace in a variety of guises: square, as if inviting a sustained campaign from unknown and unknowing enemies; rectangular, in surreptitious imitation of the snake, rising sheer and uneven with one layer superimposed upon another like a mountain; a hemisphere, which resembles the arch of the sky; a sphere, in semblance of the moon; a Pythagorean cube; or even a jumble of incongruous and incoherent forms and stuff — mountains, animals, plants or geometrical concepts. How I love to fashion my palace as an endless ruin, not just as a single city but an entire region, a continent laid waste by war, disaster, unforgiving seasons, earthquakes and landslides, epidemics or millennial decadence. In this way I can put into my palace every form and its simulation, with statues and scattered limbs that tell tales of horror and love, flights and supplications, all fractured tales, like words driven from their long-established syntactic homes; flamboyantly decorated façades consort with wastelands, castles, fortresses and keeps, the defences left over from absurd and senseless wars, unstable and perilous pinnacles set up on weak and dilapidated foundations, tapestries of gold eaten away by moths, oak chests rotten with worms, alongside drawing-rooms that have been quite untouched, the glass of their windows restored after centuries as if by a miracle, amid a wondrous ruin of wrecked walls on which the fragments of scorched frescoes may still be seen. Weaponry from every century, covered in rust; coats of arms that once commanded the world's dread now covered over with ivy, colonnades meant for deities beside which only a giant hand remains, recalling a monument not yet quite forgotten.

The fountains have dried up, but water still lingers on the roads; the aqueducts are overrun with hanging gardens that threaten to drag them down. But at the centre of this ancient ruin stands the equally boundless royal palace which I watch over with my laugh and my sighs. I have no idea whether the ruins are a simulation, a defence, an apotheosis or a coat of arms, but these things give my kingliness a rugged secular quality that both disturbs and cheers me, as if my power extended even over the dead, and the cemeteries obeyed me; bones still clothed in ancient armour. What literature was written by those who lived within these ruined walls? What their music? What trumpets sounded? I listen to the silence which has preserved the murdered forms of ancient melody, and I know that the wreckage of the centuries lies at my feet. At night a moon, eternally full, sends rocks flying down and dislodges loose bricks; the fury of a rainstorm washes frescoes away, an illegible papyrus shrivels up and is consumed.

With a single movement of my mind, I close the countless windows of the royal palace and decide when night should fall, for colours obey me just as much as the light. I think of lamps all aflame, the angry eruptions of torches spitting sparks, like comets held captive in a bracket on the wall, I think of marble within which only angels would dare to dance, stiffly cold and flashy in their robes of stone, cloaked in rock; of different kinds of wood that embody the forest's dense luxuriance and also the primeval knowledge of a kingly style, hallowed by the harshness of centuries — see where a drop of fresh resin follows a fissure carved out by the tolling of the millennial year. I think of draperies able to create of their own accord the wind that twists them into the most rarefied and fantastic shapes; windows that open wide at the touch of breezes scented with spring and secret dungeons, with flowers and decay. Mirrors artfully framed in gold and quick to reflect every shape and every shadow, the shock of bunches of non-existent flowers, capable of every savagery of scent, every impiety of colour, in the shapes of animals or human organs, with blossoms that suggest they are intoxicating or poisonous. My clocks mark the time in a manner that is sometimes musical with the rhythm of a drum, or with whisperings, breathing or sighs, the tolling of bells, the ringing and pealing of bells, carillons, the gambols of imaginary animals, the clangour of halberds, trumpets, melodic trills on violins, the vapour blown out by whales, the sparking of torches, the deep vibration of gentle cavernous voices, the murmuring of elves, the cunning woodworms of ticking seconds; and because I provide my clocks with the time they measure out like skilful tailors, they mark eras that are contemporary or prehistoric or which relate to an incomprehensible future, times of high drama, or times of joy; I can set the time of weddings, and births, and then slow down these celebrations until they are as listless as farewells. I change the location of corridors, the figure in the marbles, or the legends depicted on tapestries; I expel gods and goddesses, other deities I create and approve; I beg a wall to repeat a tale for me that would reconcile me to sleep, or otherwise set over all of this a lucid silence that is respectful and motionless. Although my power over time is absolute, as befits a complete and mature kingliness, eventually the moment is reached when my thoughts take on the shapes and colours of the night; the scents it inspires are both fresh and beyond interpretation, tender and deadly; I look out over the ruins and marvel at the columns made enormous by their shadows, I caress the abstracted breast of the moon, and suddenly extinguish the torches and the lamps at my back. The marbles are snuffed out, and I no longer know whether the walls and the tapestries are telling me the stories I wish to hear. The clocks become subdued, hesitant. What time should they tell, what rhythms and what favoured moments should they strike and how display their skills as clowns, jesters and embellishers of death? Weddings or wars? Liturgy or games? I look about me, I concentrate my gaze: I can make out the infinite stretches covered with ivy, and with a thought's breath remove the flowers which hang down over the sloping façades of a building that is about to collapse — a temple, place of human sacrifice or a royal palace. I lean out, and shake myself: why am I so different now from that moment this morning when I sent out my laughter to survey the royal palace? I race up to a large terrace, and from there hold sway over the light and the magnificence of all the devastation; I signal to the clocks to be silent, I put the frogs to death and the crickets to sleep; I prick up my ears, my gaze is all-seeing, I enlarge my nostrils, waiting to pick up in the night some sign of that unique form which I have not thought about before.

The question which in some way overrides the inventions of my mind, and which, moreover, is included in them, is this: are subjects essential to the concept, to the very definition of kingliness? I have described the eagle's prey as his "subjects", but is this way of speaking fitting and pertinent? Do such creatures become the eagle's subjects by way of an all-embracing definition, or does the celestial ferocity of his wings make them so? Or are they his subjects only in the moment between their choosing death and their death itself? Or does their status as subjects coincide with their becoming his flesh and blood, in their flight within the eagle's guts and veins? What happens in this hierarchical world when the eagle sleeps? Does he still have subjects then? Or are there spaces within kingliness, interruptions and moments of decline? An absolute kingliness cannot admit interruptions in the condition of being a subject or in relation to anything that is not directly involved in kingliness; everything, therefore, is subject to kingliness, always and for all time. Thus the eagle exercises power over rocks, over lizards and musical notes. But are there then hierarchies within the condition of being a subject? Can an animal that is preyed upon be considered a subject and share that same designation with a toy trumpet that lies forgotten on a farmyard floor by a drowsing child? Let us suppose that there are no hierarchies here; in that case kingliness will find itself faced with an extended servitude, an endless expanse of obedience and subjection. This quality of being a subject will be close to kingliness, and will add up to this — the World that confronts the King with its subject status will have become an institution that gives form to a particular mode of kingliness. The world will no longer be simply a federation of things, but an existence, a co-existence, an essence, and a mental space; it will be everything that is not kingliness; and so, dialectically, it will be amenable to a dignity that is equal to kingliness. But if we imagine that there *is* a hierarchy here, would we not see kingliness over-extended, with marshes or deserts it cannot reach, which it almost touches but then rejects, either out of disdain or distraction. And so might these lesser classes of subjects, the inferior and weaker ones, then reconfigure themselves as alternatives, in a natural conspiracy removed from the consortium of absolute kingliness?

In consequence then, can we eliminate "the subject", such as it is? Kingliness marshals its standards in the desert, or rather the desert itself is nothing but a creation of kingliness, like my columns, or the restless clocks. So is it possible that the total abstraction, the simulated concreteness of objects brought into being by my mind, could exhaust the subtle tyranny and presumption of my absolute and eternal power? Can non-existent objects be both subject to me and yet nothing more than the substantive, ephemeral limbs of my power? I can increase the number of moons threefold, bind rivers together into the coherent image of a lake; I can choose whether I sleep and dream of a world that is incongruent with this world, or dream them both at the same time and then examine my authority or rule over this impossibility, even though this "impossible", having been created by me, cannot be different from me or inimical to my power. Or I can conjure up an independently existing world that retains the condition of being subject, and is thus not kingly, and thus not born from my imagining. I can delude myself with a nothingness that is so well formulated — in the game in which I determine both the rules and the exceptions to the rules — that it is a nothing other than a something that exists. Of course, I can lie to myself. But are these then the options for kingliness — nothingness or dissimulation? Or can my deception make me different from myself so that a part of me abdicates and loosens its grip on power and becomes subject to another part? A rebellion within myself? Or can I delegate kingliness to myself and so become either a subject, reluctantly, or a rebel?

I look out again, in the night which, in accordance with the hour, takes on the different phases of the moon; I peer into the ruins; I listen; I run through all the possible rustlings of nature and animals, the landslips, or the cracking of rocks. But this evening I do not hear the flute. Or perhaps it is an ocarina, anyway some little thing, a sorry note. A mouth organ. This sound is so laughably tiny, so thin, aside from being quite ordinary, with its unremarkable tune, and yet I cannot help trying to catch a note of it. Perhaps an event such as this could break apart the cohesion of my kingliness? Or could it be its coronation? The first time I happened to hear this sound was quite recently I suppose, that is if I can detach it from my continual violations of time. But it *is* "recent", for I first heard this sound of a harmonica at a moment during that period when I was not in control of time, when perhaps it used not to belong to me. Let me repeat those words: perhaps it used not to belong to me — words which seem to me completely without meaning and yet I delight in them. The sound of the ocarina broke my nightly routine. It was a ridiculous melody but also unbearable. I created a calm night, and waited, and eventually I heard again that feeble, metallic note. So look at me now, walking amid the ruins, pushing aside the ivy and hiding behind columns, disguising myself with the colour of the stone, hiding the moon so I can advance, stealthily, cautiously. Look. Outside the picturesque ruins of a late-empire palace: an outline. I ask myself: Man or Beast? It is slender, graceful, quite tiny. Does it have a name? I listen to it without pleasure, but why deny that my interest in this being is of another kind? For the thought of it had never crossed my mind. I remain motionless like a ruin among the ruins, making myself be patient, and elemental, like a flowering plant, a saxifrage; I assume roots. The sound, which could be the whistling of a reed or a breath passing through gapped teeth or across the edge of a leaf, goes on and on. I draw the moon closer, and try to comprehend the lineaments of a being that whistles. But it stays hidden and although it does not seem to fear the dazzling light of the night, since it makes no move to hide itself, I am not able to make out its shape, if it has one. I wonder whether the sound is a cry, hence whether there is a pair of them, or if there are others of the same species or kind. I do not think so. Is this then, whatever it is, a solitary creature? Where does it come from? Look, I am lying, though I do not see why or how I am lying, nor who I am lying to.

There came a moment when I decided to cease wielding my kingliness among the triangles and cubes in my mind. Instead I looked for comparisons, for likenesses, and just happened to invent the relentless beating of the eagle's wings, the lion's scent and the slimy elongation of the serpent. They were nothing other than me, but through them I found a means to recognise myself, to replicate myself. In this way I discovered the delights of other forms. The eagle resembled me but was not me. Together we shared the same image. But the eagle, the lion and the serpent, once imagined, did not stop being themselves. It was at that moment, in order to keep a close watch over them, that I created the concept of subjects. Previously I spoke of prey, victims and nourishment. But from the moment I thought of "subjects", I began to fear for my kingliness. It was then that I heard the ocarina. Once again I am lying. When I began to create the royal palace — and particularly the ruins — I built them in the hope that this simulation of history would attract beings that were unaware of my duplicity, and that the singularities of its forms, the proficiency of its passageways might entice, from heaven knows where, living beings I had not thought of. When I heard the whistling, I felt a horror of myself. Had I travelled so far from myself in order to find this other? It was at that point that I began the ambushes. In the daytime I circled around seeking traces of excrement, footprints, a hand or a paw print that would give me some clues as to the origin of this unknown sound. I compelled the rocks to remain unchanging, smooth and impervious, because I wanted to persuade myself that they were in league with the other. Why was I lying? Had I such a hunger for this new subject that I was prepared to renounce my whole world, by withdrawing into myself, like some infinitely senile creator of animals, in order to surrender my kingdom to a small and elusive being? I thought that the constant nature of the place would allow the creature with the whistle to move around more easily, and build for itself covered shelters or refuges of various dimensions, and I inspected these artificial resting-places every day to see whether it had spent time in any of them. I made the rhythm of days and nights slow and repetitive, supposing that it was a shy thing and easily frightened; unperturbed, I took control of the moon's journeying, and welded together the constellations. The whistle was absent night after night; then I heard it again. I will not describe the care and skill I employed, nor how I demeaned myself in order to draw close to this nocturnal enigma. I caught a glimpse of its outline, the shadow of a shadow; I stood quite still. Perhaps I wished for no more than this. But even though I find the recollection of what I see in my mirrors unbearable, I still wanted to see it, though I did not dare to hope to touch it. I realised that the creature did not always whistle. The disturbed grass and displaced stones spoke to me of its haphazard expeditions. I found the grass. Blades pulled out with meticulous neatness, stalks cut back, dried and set down on a stone as smooth as slate. A drawing; before me rose up the columns with which I had hoped to seduce it, and which it had re-created with strange mastery in this composition made of grasses. A draughtsman, a seeker after images. The design, however, was singularly diminished, and made one think of a very small creature, pathologically precise; I feared for him in this labyrinth of ruins, so I multiplied the soft grasses and gently comforting vines. I did not dare leave a message, though a sign added to his signs would have been enough. A useless precaution; not once did it return to this place. In another spot I found strange markings like tattoos on the rocks, often just sketched in though sometimes finished off with exceptional skill, then abandoned. There was something distinctly generous in his behaviour, and I wondered whether he also participated in the prodigality of royalty. I found other signs, infrequently and some distance away — stones dislodged for some particular effect, drawings of stone on stone, and finally images drawn with a black substance on the brightness of the rock. This creature evidently loved mannered forms, and wished to embellish the beautiful while discomposing its rules. His touch was felicitous and nervous. Well, I could not hide myself any longer. I wanted to amaze him, to fascinate him with gestures of wild splendour, and so I unleashed my baroque disposition; I rearranged the nights all over again; I let loose thirty-two moons into a sky that towered thirty-two times higher than before; from an amalgam of the constellations I fashioned a nocturnal sun, a cold sun that was capable only of providing light and darkness at the same time; I devised ruins of infinite complexity, and daubed frescoes on the desert, created statues that spoke, revolving mirrors, flowers that sang; I left extravagant and impossible foods at the corners of ruined streets, lit fires and brought on sudden local showers; I set up dancing machines. I threw open the doors of the royal palace, then built others that looked like triumphal arches, so that he would know that at any time he could approach me. Dazzling suns created a perpetual yet gentle summer, and everywhere I let waters flow, and slender trunks and beneficial herbs rise up. I agree, not everything was in the best of taste, but was it not also true that I wanted to demote this absolute being, whose whistle had become quite indispensable to me and had insidiously pervaded my days? I thought that I glimpsed him in the daytime, when something both minute and stealthy crept soundlessly through the grass. How laboriously I tried to ensure he was unaware that I had seen him. I even once heard him whistling in the middle of the day; perhaps I fascinated him. I came across other drawings and saw them as suggestions for changes to be made. I complied, I chose to do so, and as a gesture of my compliance showed him noisily how I had carried out what I had construed to be his wishes. I, kingliness itself, was submissive.

I added numerous storeys to my royal palace, created sounds and perfumes to waft through them; every morning my anxious laughter fluttered through the gardens; I also uttered a cry of sorrow, placing no hope in his gentleness, but instead trying to provoke his fury; I gave my voice the scents of every imaginable prey; I became flesh and fruit and resin. In the end I came out of the palace and went out to meet him. I did not try to surprise the creature any longer, by crouching in hiding; instead, with devious attentions I aimed to seduce him, beguile him and captivate him. In all my purples and my gold, resplendent in my bucklered armour and dazzling with my jewellery and rings, bound with my sword-belt loose like the heroes of the constellations, and cloaked in purple, crimson and gold, with glittering bracelets. I walked in the gardens and covered myself with eyes whose distant gaze affected the magnificent indifference of kings. I declaimed poetry as loudly as I was able; I arranged for music to accompany my words that was in turn noble and philosophical, then common and sentimental; I even imitated the very sound of the creature's whistle, and this seemed to me a particularly cunning ruse.

I pranced about like a peacock; I turned slowly in circles, as tall as a mountain, visible from many miles away, and whirled around swathed by my cloak; I set my buckles jingling, kicked out and struck lightning from my spurs. I turned myself into a horse the size of a massive boulder that galloped across the plains, roaring and neighing. I drew swords and loosed lances; I created giants which I then killed and dispersed into clouds. I surrounded myself with trumpets and violins; I moved among actors, masks, puppets, circus animals and creatures with startling deformities; I laughed like a man unhinged, slapping my massive metal calves. I shone as brilliantly as a gong as large as the sun, and was able to outstare it. Dogs ran from me, I pretended to race after them, shouting continually and looking always about me, in search of the other. More than once I caught a glimpse, but then no more; very small he was, and very fast. And nothing could make me believe that he was the slightest bit entranced by all this crazy pomp.

I covered myself with blood, which excites dogs and sharks; I dragged myself to the point of death, leaving traces of pus in my wake; I filled the world with my groans and made the constellations shrink with disgust at the cacophony of my words; I uttered wild soliloquies detailing my wholly specious anguish; I officiated at extraordinary funerals for non-existent relatives and wrote a sequence of sonnets to a woman I loved, now dead, proclaiming them at the top of my voice from the terrac; with dishevelled hair and my doublet all unbraced I ranted against the injustice of kings, urged my fellows citizens to rebel and railed against man's exploitation of his fellow man; I published a pamphlet which I distributed to every corner of my gardens among the ruins, even up to the steps to the palace; I simulated marriages; I presented to the people a fiancée made of alabaster and tow; I extracted hurrahs from the silent stones while countless torches covered my palace by night and day; I dazzled the sun with fireworks. I ordered acts of mourning and acts of penitence, and experimented with the nocturnal colours of black, deep red and dark blue, together with the solemn melodies of liturgy; I raised up churches dedicated in my name, and called upon myself with heart-rending homilies, while all the time I was watching for that slight, fortuitous figure, seemingly absent-minded, else not interested or unaware. In an instant I stilled gargantuan orchestras to silence in order to take his crude and intermittent whistle by surprise. It was then that I threw out nets, became a bird, an animal of prey, an impetuous dog, a serpent, lion, eagle, cat and kite; I dragged the ruins together to form a trap; but what have I ever found save a hint of ridicule, and even that not deliberate, and this is the awful thing — nothing but the mockery of indifference, pure and simple. Only once was there an outline, half cat, half human, at other times only a colour, perhaps plumage or some lithe outer form that mimicked the appearance of an animal.

My royal palace is ready; my countless clocks mark every possible time, the doors and windows are all wide open. Having leant out of the window, I am now languishing in the indolence of a night without end. The anxious desperation with which I have hunted this uncouth sound is at an end, and although I am not discouraged, I have the sense of having made some slight mistake, which cannot fail to disturb my nocturnal meditations. I wonder if he wants me to go elsewhere, or enter the nothingness that I myself envisaged before I was beguiled by the eagle's allure. I turn to look out over the palace with indifference. Provided the order is clear, I will obey; I will obey *you*, my subject or my king.

SIMULATIONS

I inhabit an ingeniously furnished hallucination, and marvel at the skill with which its walls have been simulated as protection against the night. I know that the walls are one with the night, and with the wind and the rain, and that, within this simulation, which encompasses everything, there are limits which cannot be transgressed. I know that at a certain moment during the night there appears to be some kind of beast, which loathes me. I tame it with a symbolic gesture of my hands, a gesture I think I have inherited from past experience. I am sitting in the centre of a room and between me and the wall I have set up an elaborate cultural fiction: a picture. I marvel at it, though I can never possibly understand what it represents. And the representation is bountiful; its colours masquerade as animals, a love scene or an ancient Egyptian triumphal procession. I can hear the sound of copper trumpets coming from the street, unless it is coming from the very heart of this image. I study my hands, my perfect hands. They are very unusual, but as far as I am aware they are unable to represent anything and can only perform from an unwritten script, but the performance is so effective that it is quite moving, although difficult too. I wonder if the simulation is so dense and integrated that it covers the whole area of the city, if it continues beyond me, penetrating into nothingness and civilising it with a finely judged arrangement of geometric shapes and colours. Why was the decision taken to simulate colours? What a wonderful trick! My clothes, the only aspect of me that is, and knows itself to be deceitful, glitter from within the frame; I feel sure that the painting is watching me. I presume I am to be party to some hidden conspiracy. I ask myself whether I am required to be a fundamental collaborator in the invention of this world. I am bound to lie but I am unsure at what point in my argument: when I make the decision to create something, when I enjoy the result, or when I make it clear that my creation is a simulation? I imagine that this room is the inner room of a castle, that on the lower floor my servants and my hired killers take turns switching roles; I listen; someone has struck up a conversation about war and bloodshed, another person is relating anecdotes about sordid love affairs. I decide that I have won a war; I correct myself, preferring a long drawn-out and revolting tale of skirmishing and ambush. I think I could take pity on these shadows; I give them names without thinking about it and often specifically so as to confuse them. If I listen very hard, I can hear their agitated, anxious footsteps, and the unpleasant clamour of their voices; I smile. If, at this moment, I should lean out of a window, I would discover whether, beyond this room, beyond the castle, there stretches a city, a place filled with terror and crime, or whether my invention has already extended this space into a desert, and in that case, whether the desert existed before my castle in the false time of simulations, or whether it was brought into being by an intelligent and irrevocable act of destruction. I wonder if the difference between the two is only a matter of presentation. My hands are so elegant, but I cannot ignore the possibility that, in some respects, I am a monster of cruelty. I won't rise from my chair, I won't look out, I won't open the window; some odour might creep indoors — how embarrassing — that foul animal smell which belongs to no animal. I recall that ten days' journey from here there is an endless cave which shelters on its infinite ledges the tails, eyes, genitals, roars, death-rattles, fur, wings, scales and fins of countless possible animals. Yet sometimes one's imagination falters, and inspiration can fall away — or perhaps it's just that the tedium of this oft-repeated ritual is so distressing. I ask myself again whether I am indeed a collaborator or just a petty criminal; or simply the *magnum opus* amidst all of these simulations. Why do I recall that at this hour the castle will catch fire? But between this moment and the castle's destruction I have time to live a thousand lives, fitting one inside another, like hollow reeds or empty tombs.

My mother is dead. To be more accurate, this morning I awoke as an orphan. Memories, simulations within simulations, crowd together with unbelievable pathos. In the featureless space of my fictitious past I decided to situate the fictitious physicality of beings I once loved with a complex love, quick-tempered and full of a resentment that was hard to relinquish. This time my mother is extremely old, and has said very little for years, worn down by a hope which no fiction has ever brought to pass. The coffin's splendour cannot alleviate her error, the chief symptom of which is her wasted body. My brother has travelled here from inhospitable and exotic regions, hastening through lands populated by wild beasts and racing frantically for a thousand days, only to arrive just in time to open the coffin and look upon that beloved face, now quite unrecognisable. He throws himself into agonies of despair; I clap my hands in applause. His beautiful hair is dishevelled and all over the place; his sighs reverberate around the room. The faithful servants are more subdued, and offer him their humble support. I let the curtain fall and take my leave. It requires humility as well as artistry and deceit to make a counterfeit of one's mother, and then to revel in her death. Hers was a death lacking in any melodramatic touches; she was broken and had wasted away slowly, very slowly, absorbed in a performance that owed nothing to the inspiration of mouth nor eye, but everything to the increasing depletion of her exceptionally long body. This simulation of a mother's death involved me in another, even more subtle deception: the funeral rites. And so with priests, gods to whom sacrifice must be made, and a paradise to dispatch the dear old lady to. I explained to the priests that their business was to guarantee that the paradise where the old woman had most certainly gone, lay beyond the expanse of the sky, since it seemed appropriate to assume it was "celestial". They appeared hesitant, puzzled perhaps by the obviousness of my request. Yet I couldn't fail to doubt their ability to exist and thus to invent further states of existence. But having to invent a god, well, that was a tiresome nuisance. While my brother's grief caused distress throughout the castle, I laughed under my breath. Nothing was further from my thoughts. I respect his proficiency, and all that occurred in the castle today — death, funerals and mourning — is evidence of an exceptional intelligence. I touch him on the shoulder; he has not recovered his composure after arriving late, but he knows, naturally, just as I do, that this corpse is always here, and is always the same age as me.

For seven days, in succession, I awoke at dawn, an orphan. On the first morning I, the prince of princes, had just interred in the crypt my mother, who had been murdered by a lover she had betrayed. I became attached to this dramatic and beguiling fiction, and in the nocturnal ambience of my bed I cherish this fake memory and this artifice of a dead woman, a mother ruled by vice and passion, tormented by casual and compulsive affairs, a creature of elegant speech who wore garments of a studied gaudiness, but who was entirely resigned to the melancholy business of genitalia and always partial to transactions negotiated with her loins. In spite of this she was a marvellous mother. I do not know who my father was, and laugh at my ability to create such complex situations as I emerge from my sleep. Have I invented her, this mother, in compensation for the tired calculations of everyday inventions? I have expanded the colour boundaries of my world, and pretended that an error crept in as a result, a ruinous and shocking error. I call to mind banquets, balls, all kinds of music, flags and toasts. Despite my horror of metals, I set about creating a dagger. My innocent imagination dared to sketch out a scene of illicit intercourse, and the fine-featured but ill-starred face of my mother's final lover. His body, cut to pieces by halberds, is thrown over the castle battlements. It lies in the mud; it could be my father. In the featureless world of my past, I am always the same age as him.

This morning my mother tried to kill me; I was confined in her womb, and was reading the classics. A flame blotted out the page, and this troubled my dreams. And since it was possible for me to do so, I allowed the fire to kill my mother. Now, she is my tomb. I am enclosed within the fleshy boundaries of this dying creature and only my extreme smallness allows me the slightest comfort. I value this sepulchre a great deal, for the gracious intimations of a life that has been lost gives every part of her body an aura of infinite nobility. In its exact vastnesses wherein I find contentment, it is not the ingenuity of the tomb's architects, the rich intensity of its materials or the sumptuousness of the crowds who lean from its balconies that inspire my meditations. Rather it is because, since it is a simulation of a body, it is untouched by human hands and constitutes an infinity of flesh within whose labyrinths I may wander, amazed and fascinated, my mind bewildered by its cartography. My mother's body, I finally understand, is infinite; I realise that I am at the heart of the beyond, and remember that I have always been here, have always been born and always been dead, with no knowledge of my birth: I have been marked for ever by a maternal scar. In the end I do not know whether it was my diminutive size that gave me unlimited space, or whether the hollow body of my mother may have been designed, in effect, to be endless, and above all without skin, or limbs, nor any external form. I am within — where else could I be? This mother therefore has neither a face, nor teeth. In this respect, she resembles the sky, which, I suppose, is the hollow of a face, with the nose protruding from the other side. Some distance from me, my mother is turning from black to red, and then becomes azure; and this is when I recognise myself again, in my castle, in the middle of my bed. But today my body will be humid, all day.

My mother flees wearily through the desert, holding me close to her breast; this is a place of scrub, sand, splinters and snakes that have died from exhaustion; shifting dunes mark the sites of cities long since fallen into ruin through the ravages of time, or the remains of a camel, a relic of the last caravan to brave this empty space. The otherwise silent air is heavy with the groans of animals that have died, generation upon generation. My father will kill my mother when he catches up with her: he is a godless man and my mother knows that his bitter sadness has been passed down to me, that he has poisoned my blood. While my mother runs, I bite her on her breast, but not from hunger. This sand is made of empires, churches, warriors and lovers; my father — and I know this because he and I have the same wickedness in common — knows that this waste matter, which cannot even decompose, will bore its way into the heart of the kingdom and suffocate him; and so he should kill my mother now, before everything submits to the sand's deep quiescence. The external forms of nameless animals, those eternal assassins, smite my mother to the ground — how cleverly I have planned this dark, dead covering of sand. Father, you must be quick. My mother is dying; you surely do not want her to die without having laid your hand on her yourself, without her feeling your hatred? I try to make out my mother's face. Clutched to her breast I can just see the hollows of her nostrils, but cannot distinguish her eyes which are black and brimming with angry, impotent tears; her body has worn thin, so urgently do these protruding bones yearn to become sand, and the sky overhead, once eager to fill this ultimate desert with its radiance, now decides to snuff itself out leaving only the dull glare of comets, those rags and wisps of light. I withdraw from my mother's embrace; suddenly adult, I rise up over her body, and with all my breath shout out to my father where we are, at the same time stopping her body from moving by pressing my foot down through it until she becomes part of the sand beneath, while my father's dagger plunges in search of her mouth and eyes: I try to make him out but can only hear his killer's breath — so similar to mine.

I realise that I am an orphan, but I don't know in which sarcophagus my mother's body lies; and because she died when I was born I have no notion of her name or features. I stand in the middle of the cemetery and count the tombs of all my possible mothers. But because the tombs are all sealed I cannot recall whether each one shelters a single body or whether there may be several in each. Obviously, no names are inscribed upon them. In this way I am absolved from grieving, but not from the pain of not understanding who I am. There is a possibility that all these women were implicated in my birth, since it was so complex and dark that it might have benefited from an abundance of mothers. Or perhaps in a moment of metaphysical bravado I decide to attribute my origins to an infinite and morbid system of motherhood; and anyway, who can tell me whether the women buried here were ever alive? Is it not possible that my life was born of their death, from their original state of being dead, that is? Perhaps I owe to that process the tender feeling of gratitude I experience among these tombs, given that they remain as they are always and for ever? Yet I am certain I have no brothers; just a father, and maybe, having lain with my mother in the shadowy confines of these maternal tombs, perhaps he too does not exist. With a shrug, I take my leave.

I try to discover, from my mother on her deathbed, who my father might be. She is wrinkled and frail. I hate this face that shows no knowledge of either sorrow or joy, but is forever anxious, thoughtful and difficult. I seize her roughly by the throat and call her a whore. She looks hard at me, with a thoughtful expression. Do I suspect her of some new kind of lechery? Or more likely fraud. Can this woman really be my mother? Is she not the epitome of sterility, with her body seared by time and tightly wrapped in the elegance of a sky-blue shroud which I have known for always. I do not like this death, it is impossible, the simulation of a simulation; and while I appreciate the virtuosity of this invention, her infinite capacity for play-acting disgusts me. Why doesn't she reply? She peers at me as if she has exactly the same doubts. I do not know who my father is, but nothing can prevent me from suspecting that she does not know who my mother might be. Why are we so irreparably at odds, and why so inarguably of the same blood? Do blood relations exist between people who are not of the same blood? Between those who do not come from the same womb? Is it possible that our kinship and her motherhood can be established indirectly through hospitalisation in the same shadowy darkness? We look at each other and our mutual horror dissipates in a shared disgust, eventually becoming the hint of a laugh, or maybe it is a death-rattle. Your dying is pointless, I am already your orphan, from before the time you were born, if indeed you ever were born. Should I look elsewhere? I shall keep watch on you with a glance over my shoulder.

I have before me, on the table, a map of the war I have decided to win; I am surrounded by bitter men to whom I have assigned, in this fable I am constructing, courage and tight-lipped pride. I explain to them where they are, and that each one of them will be going to his death; I mark the place on the map with a red cross, and make a note of their name (which I have just made up). I feel proud of myself, the warriors declare themselves content, and that they feel magnificent; one of them sobs. I have provided each of them with a wife, and children too; tomorrow my city will be glorious and filled with tears, a quite special blend of triumph and disaster. From the castle window I point out, in my antiquated but convincing rhetoric, the places where the monuments to their glory will rise up. I shake my general's hand with deep emotion; his fate is to remain unburied, and in fact he is already celebrated by a stylish cenotaph in some ironically sumptuous church. At a flourish of my hand, trombones and trumpets blare, the bands troop out from magnificent doorways with disciplined frenzy and soon they will confront the Enemy. Perhaps it was not worth the effort to create so convincing an "enemy"; it would have been enough to hang pikes from the trees, to cross a few broken lances over the valiant fallen and to sow the fields with arrowheads. My forces obey me, and all those I have assigned to die will meet their death in the place allocated. Yet my taste for simulation imposes a respect for the rules, not so much of verisimilitude, an obviously contradictory concept, but the integrity of craftsmanship. Consequently, they will meet the Enemy, or rather a fragment of enmity that is skilled at being beaten, and fall as they kill; a simulation which in this case verges on allegory, a portrait of hostility in miniature. I can see flags flooding the streets of the ancient capital with their makeshift colours. Women are clutching the departing soldiers in their arms. I withdraw from the presence of those who are about to die for me, and who will spill their steaming blood on the same sand my mother's skeletal feet trampled in her flight. When I close the door all sound is hushed; I dim the sun with an unpredictable eclipse and turn to contemplate the impure white of the walls.

Around me cluster the men who will soon die in vain in the battle they are fated to lose. They will die with my name on their lips — the name I have lent them so they can think of me, given the irritating transformations my face undergoes — their corpses hacked to pieces by swords, and no one will gather up their bodies; crows and jackals, who now are sleeping deep within the castle dungeons, will venture out to devour their pitiful remains. I watch their faces attentively, faces that seem unique, and seek in their hollowed eyes the fear of senseless slaughter and inescapable death. These men who have reached their end are only just about capable of uttering a careless disloyal prayer; their appearance is abject and withdrawn, they entrust their widows to me, and their orphaned children too, who, as they know, will be left to the merciful ravishment of the victors. I comfort them with a kindly smile and a gesture of my hand, half priestly, half princely. It is I who will put their widows and children to the sword, should they escape the slaughter. But there is little doubt they will perish in the flames, for in the expectation of just such a day I had the entire city constructed from wood, and all of it tinder-dry; my castle, meanwhile, is no more than a collage that simulates brick. Should I myself experience any of the anguish of aggression, or quake at the enemy's attack, the assassin's knife at my throat? But why prolong the agony of these bodies, these bodies of nothingness? I turn, and half out of disgust, half from boredom, walk away.

In this city today people flock in from the surrounding countryside in great hordes, gamblers, whole circuses, animals of every colour, athletes, story-tellers, jesters, priests from three religions, newly-weds, old lechers, young lads on their first visit to a place of vice, exotic merchants, drunks, drug addicts, musicians and quacks. The crowd is so dense that the city streets are a puree of humanity, stinking of sweat and urine, and a great racket sounds from everywhere. I could wipe out the whole city with an earthquake or a plague, or a conflagration, an attack by brigands, a heavenly visitation or a flood. I try out these forms of death one after another; a third of the houses crash to the ground after a tremor of the raging earth, another third I consign to the flames and the last third to the waters; any who escape will either be killed by the brigands or laid waste by the plague; in the end a host of angels will erase the very name of the city from history and render the site of its foundations as smooth as stone that has been polished by water. From the same fiction I will save a fool who, with fanciful lack of accuracy, will regale me with tales of the end of a great city, and of its days of glory and magnificence. Then I shall even wipe away my dear fool.

Insurgents are close on my heels. It's night. With a handful of faceless followers I am swiftly following a path that runs between forests and ravines, not particularly innovative, but why should I continuously strive, and at all costs, for a tiresome originality? I must get to the border, and am aware that one of my followers is familiar with the route, but I know too that concealed amidst the scattered escort accompanying me is a traitor. The rebels have killed my wife and children and put my palace to the torch, and now they are putting my ministers on trial; already they have set up the gallows. We run on through the night, our horses slithering on the damp grass and loose stones. We glimpse a few houses lit by faint lamps. Across the border allies are waiting for me, with weapons and soldiers; if I survive, they will restore me to the throne. I turn to one of the men in my company. "You, you are the traitor," I say to this fellow, and he admits it and offers up his throat; at a sign from me one of my followers cuts it quickly. I find the rhetoric of this whole business intolerable. I approach the border, and, to the despair of my companions, cross over and continue to ride past our allies; I shall write a letter of resignation. This announcement of mine sets the bells pealing through the night; an angel appears in the form of a comet. In my lost capital the rebels weep with belated emotion.

I intrigue against myself. My rebel side and my loyal side face off against one another, like mirror images, but differing nevertheless: we are different in the way we speak, in our nervous tics, in the colour of our eyes and how we dress — I am dark and melancholy, my other is garish and brash. In my rebel role I pore over the plans of the palace, and put to the test the loyalty of those servants who have access to the sovereign's secret rooms; I research daggers and poisons (he has no idea how his dog came to die). As sovereign, I have assigned a spy to follow the rebel closely; I wear a coat of mail, and make myself immune to poisons by taking small doses of them every day. I change rooms every night; every week I kill the servants who have learned the layout of the castle. As rebel, I scour the countryside to sniff out any popular discontent and whisper subversive messages hinting at future prosperity in the innocent ears of the poor and alienated. I hoard weapons in caves and train peasants in archery. I create fake coats of arms, promise noble titles to the ignorant and the gullible; I have learned all the routes that can be taken by night, and how to ride for hours in absolute silence. I gather noxious herbs on the wild mountainsides, and study the constellations and the phases of the moon for signs of the right moment to revolt. As sovereign, I pack the country with gallows and inflict terrible agonies with white-hot iron; I raze villages and take the sons of the poor as hostages. I grant dissidents the honour of bearing arms, and send them off to die in inaccessible regions of no consequence which do not even exist. I have flooded the countryside with spies and built fortresses on the tops of all the mountains; I have scattered snakes in the places where poisonous herbs grow. I have shifted the constellations so that their oppositions and conjunctions are no longer valid, and have made eclipses occur more frequently; I have transformed the animals of the night into ferocious beasts and filled the landscape around the villages with such cries of lamentation and distress that no one dares to venture out against the unknown knight except the only one who knows how to kill him. I have cut the valleys off from each other by means of a deadly trail of pestilence. As rebel, I have discovered all the underground passages and descended, through one cave after another, to the centre of the Earth; I have summoned up all the dead and made them my allies by promising them a scrap of life in the hereafter; I have also prepared legions of ghosts and stiff mummies. I have learned how to manage plagues and stampede wild animals. I light fires at a distance and am able to swoop down on the sovereign's city from a great height and spy on him through its walls. As sovereign I have summoned the hierarchies of the blessed dead, those serene connoisseurs of endless afternoon teas having become absorbed into an inspirationally musical existence, they are gifted virtuosi on harp and lute. I have signed up the seraphim and bribed the archangels; their dazzling holy weapons extend an impenetrable canopy over my entire city, palace and body. Unless I am deceived by the certainty of being right, God himself is on my side, and out of an odd kind of generosity and leniency, shows me the proof of it with miracles, such as the sudden flowering of red roses or spontaneous cures for family members, the resurrection of that dog and a suddenly clear sky that allows me to see the danger bent on striking me from a great height. My armour has been doubled in strength by dint of learned spells and there is no chink in it that would let through an arrow; daily rituals allow me to maintain my privileged relationship with the justice of the elements, the requirements of saints and, finally, the majesty of God. I have filled the palace with individuals who resemble me, in their features or in their voice, or else in their conversation and convictions, so that I am the only one to know who I am among so many, and anyone who catches a distant glimpse of my face does not know whether they are aiming at me or at one of my doubles. As rebel I enrol in the enemy's crack troops, I am the enemy in its entirety — I understand all the secrets of absolute enmity. I am not the sovereign's annihilation, I am nothing less than annihilation itself. Where I am, not even God would dare set foot, unless he were defeated and bound in chains. From my citadel I control the night, the beginning and end of time, the dead and the final eclipse. As sovereign I have enlisted myself, along with all those who resemble me, in the barracks at the centre of the world, where I dwell alongside and inside my god. I radiate the light of his consummate weaponry, and with him and through his grace I share power over his dead and his suns, the beginning and end of time, the radiance of flames, justice brought about by disease and the mark left by the thunderbolt. Enclosed within the god's dazzling capsule and misshapen in this impregnable armour, I hold the other at bay; he will not dare venture here unless he has been bound tight and yoked to my triumphal chariot. As rebel, I will rise up against God and tempt him down to the glittering destiny of the lower depths; as sovereign I will fall upon the other so as to reveal to him the orderly ecstasy of light.

Sometimes I open up my storehouse of wives, that silent confusion of faces I am forever creating and destroying; I fashion for myself a companion for my wanderings through the night, a mother for the children I am afraid of losing, a disloyal, secretive woman. Mouths, genitals, saliva, nails, all is confused. I come across traces of hair in my fictitious house, footprints that await a foot to make them; a finger that does not exist leaves marks in the dust upon a table. Solitary meals eaten facing a chair whose emptiness is no less fictitious than the body I have placed in it. In the hallway, ornaments made out of syllables and hands hang on the wall; I move my arm so that it mimics them, and imagine the reverential bows of respectful courtiers. Sometimes I kill her.

I crowd the clear, blank sky with gods, like trinkets. Everywhere is a fluttering, dazzling mass. An abundance of breath hidden in the interstices between objects. Flying insects with elongated faces, strange marvels. A sweat of blood seeps out of a stone fissured in the likeness of a face; with a flick of my thumb and forefinger I call up my supporters — I love their bowed heads and hopeless gullibility. To amuse the others: look, here is someone who dies and then rises again. I invent obscenity and create obscene deities, all hair and flesh; I watch the faithful in all their dark depravity and teach them their rhythm; they follow my lead and then disappear. I fashion a sanctuary from a bubble, leading to an endless pilgrimage; I create the repulsively sick and infect them with the ironic leprosy of "the miracle". Those who have been raised from the dead die again, the paralysed collapse, the drowned take to drink. The deaf mute, miraculously healed, will bear false witness, the man with the withered hand will take his knife to the throat of the woman who had an issue of blood and is now made whore.

The first sanctuary is sinister and luxurious; the only visible light comes from the roughness of hard stone or polished metals to be found in the delicate shapes of wrought metalwork and balustrades. This sanctuary will be sufficient to hold ten thousand gods. Each one will be made to squat in a porphyry shrine suspended from a small gold lamp-chain, or set into openings in the tabernacles.

I have designed tabernacles with six, twelve or twenty-four such cells: here I am thinking about gods who find mates and have offspring together and gradually spread throughout the world, even while they are crushed by the despair of not being worshipped. A cosmic crisis reduced to the scale of the bedroom. Here is a sanctuary for six hexagonal gods; each god is composed of an amalgam of six others, each has six faces, six semblances of omnipotence, six miracles and six special illnesses — to these gods I sometimes assign followers; sometimes I don't. On drearier evenings, I hang them up in the sky, all glittering and multi-coloured. This sanctuary is for gods who are only presumed to exist, and consists of a huge dome with a tiny floor; from the celestial skein that hangs from the dome there emerges a whole generation of gods who fly around the dome's lantern, while others drift slowly down to the wicker chairs of the faithful. The floor itself is so thickly covered with gods that it is not possible to walk on it without squashing some of them, resulting in a prodigious visceral mush. Over here is a pocket sanctuary which houses one god at a time, but it's still cosy and friendly. It consists, as you can see, of a bag, one side of which is coarse and rigid and against which the god can rest his back. This god can be used in a variety of ways: it can be sold or even left behind deliberately in railway stations, or in those places where one changes camels. In the eye at the end of an extremely tall, upright needle there dwells another god; from a ball I thread through this world of needles, and the gods in each one nod and chat to one another from one eye to the next. This sanctuary is a cube whose top can be opened: it contains a mixture for making gods, a dough of fine consistency, nicely mixed so that it may be easily laid out as required; in cylinders along the walls, meanwhile, a number of eyes are stored, even triangular eyes, which are deeply frightening, should anything exist to be frightened.

This sanctuary is actually an armoury for the gods of war, the gods of vendettas, of anger and dissent; it was a birthday gift from some principled churchmen. Here is a device for compressing the gods, who have become widely dispersed, and for reducing them to a ball of truly marvellous matter. This is the place where it is possible to be either the One God or the non-god: as you can see, it is a snuff box, made from a highly polished substance that is like a mirror.

I take the decision to act as a deity myself; I create constellations and blueprints for vast underworlds and classify cosmic catastrophes; I have followers, whom I condemn, and opponents whom I save. I listen to blasphemies and set them aside; prayers irritate me only a little; I cook up miracles so that they are as aggravating and challenging as possible. I raze to the ground my crowded sanctuaries, just on a malicious whim; I fall in love with the baroque, then cease to love it. I mix stars and planets together and extract from them a riotous mass of light. By this light I read the *Daily Deceiver*; into the obituary columns I slip my own name, which I have obviously just made up on the spur of the moment. To be absolutely precise, *all* the names in the obituaries are mine, although they are only a tiny fraction of the names I could make up, which would be enough to fill all the possible obituaries in all the possible newspapers I could ever invent. To my priests I grant, then deny, the ability to perform miracles; I involve them in, and release them from, the delights of debauchery; I want them to enjoy both poverty and opulence. Sometimes I treat myself to a god-partner and drunkenly play a grubby hand of cards with him, a game of constellations and cemeteries, sanctuaries and monastic orders. Finally I invent a devil and entrust the world to him, and find myself briefly distracted by his torments and slander. And then I wipe everything out, using dawn as a cloth. If I make the gods my courtiers then I am the supreme god, but this one is impetuous, this one thoughtful, this one cunning, another is captivating and yet another discourteous. And how noisy they are! I dispatch them towards worlds they will never find, and holes into which they will disappear for ever.

I can destroy a constellation with fire, ageing it abruptly by means of a sudden explosion or a muffled implosion; this drains the night of every trace of light, blinding each star with another star and forcing them into a mutual confrontation, until finally they dissolve into the nothingness in which they have incautiously come to rest. To put out all of them, all together, one need only flick this switch.

Confined in prison I reach out and feel the walls with my hand, they surround me; I discover mould, dead insects and marks left by other prisoners. A faint light filters down from high overhead. I have found no doors, nor fissures that might suggest a way out through the stone. It appears that I have walled myself up inside this prison, or alternatively I think of myself as being completed by the prison which fits around me like a suit. There is no sign of any other prisoners, and I receive no word concerning the crime that has caused me to be imprisoned; more specifically, nothing leads me to suppose that I ever committed such a crime, or even that my imprisonment is a punishment. I travel swiftly through space and am quickly convinced that it is effectively endless. Given my situation, it is pointless to struggle, or to call for help or for the reason for my punishment to be made clear. In a time that is my own, a time will come when I will be nothing but my own prison.

Chained up at the bottom of a circular pit, I make out a dull sky in the distant opening above. The earth slides away around me, the stench of marshes chokes me; hairless animals with faces I have not finished off trample over my body. Sometimes the sounds of voices I cannot understand reach me from above. A bar fixed into the ancient masonry of the well supports a metal cup full of water to which I can just about reach with my mouth. When night steals over the well, tiny creatures fly close to my face, judging from the frantic, senseless squealing. I open my mouth and swallow them, in their looping trajectory, whole. I really notice the absence of fine French wine.

With a few careless gestures, part guilty and part indifferent, they seal up my narrow cell. A nod from the finely robed executioner signals my farewell to the world. I have listened to the adieu of passing footsteps, heard the creak of doors receding further and further in the distance; utter silence falls, like dark shadows. The sentence is such that it reduces me, slowly, very slowly, to excrement; I will stockpile all my urine and dump my faeces; I will sleep on top of it all. My disjecta, as it solidifies, will raise me up until I am crushed against the ceiling. My garments will decay, and I will be left clothed only in shit. Slowly my body will be translated into my filth, and will itself exude from my basest orifices; and thus my body will become my own prison, a prison from which I shall be able to leak out. The last of the urine, cloudy and salty, will seep through the walls and with eyes of excrement discover the world anew.

The Judge is despicable but exceptionally shrewd; he points to various ominous objects, one by one: pliers, stakes, knives, poison, ropes, crosses, pincers, nail-tearers and eye-gougers. His language is a mystery to me but his authority, like the brutish movements of his hands, is indisputable. Huge books are spread open on the table and he leafs through them with furious haste. Standing at the foot of his judicial desk are the Inquisitors, Executioners, Torturers, Prosecutors and Prevaricators, together with witness statements, both fake and genuine, and several sheaves of paper. I notice that he has ten hands, and twenty eyes, and that his spittle clogs up his syllables and scrambles the sound of his voice. I know that he is trying to establish that certain heinous crimes have been committed so as to persuade me of my guilt. He reconstructs my life, day by day, and notes down all the details of my abhorrent criminality. Anger and fury spread over the faces of his assistants, and it is only the knowledge of the novel tortures to which I will be subjected that restrains them from tearing me to pieces on the spot. I have no idea what any of my crimes might be, but because each one is catalogued in the tribunal's judicial library I am sure they will apply to me in every regard. To help them I am constantly extending my past, and yet even though I have back-dated my birth some crimes still evade me, and I am not quite able to take on the whole gamut of punishments. Therefore, I shall make my life eternal.

With a wild and unpredictable movement I have overturned the guards' bench, snatched a sword from the inattentive hands of someone nearby and savagely attacked the man who was restraining me. I leapt through the window and here I am fleeing through the city that is a chaotic mass of ruined timber structures and reeking urinals.

I leap astride a horse and race towards the gates, slipping under the portcullis as it falls; the arrows miss me, and I end up somewhere in the marshes that encircle the city. No one will ever dare follow me here with all the dragons and flying snakes, but I will never risk leaving this watery maze of reeds, this labyrinth of stagnant lakes, malarial and ridden with disease. The horse collapses. I let it die among the reeds. I will live on voles, scrawny coots and rotten berries. I lean forward and part the reeds only to make out through the mist the walls of the city that condemned me but whose people are afraid of the marshlands and of me, their sovereign.

I have escaped from my cell into another cell; I am still in the prison, but in some other part of it. Incarcerated yet difficult to find, I help the jailers in their confused search. I move from one cell to another, finding myself in the company of killers, thieves, pimps, con-men and forgers, and wherever I go I learn every detail of the skills and regrets that go with each crime. Wasted away, right down to the bone, yet sharp-eyed and agile, I take on the same dullness the warders have. I assume the noble, institutional look that is proper for an avenger. I shall move through the whole of the prison, through every floor and every room, but only because my life is infinite. In a thousand years we will all get to know each other well and yet this comedy of pursuit within the confines of this prison, all for the sake of a bureaucratic readjustment of my situation that is altogether disastrous, will never end.

I wander, guilty yet charming, through the lower depths, the city's back-streets, hiding in low dives, whore-houses and boozers; with the brim of my hat hard down over my eyes I hatch deals involving the meanest rubbish: old shoes, ragged clothes, the dentures from corpses. Depending on who's walking by I pass myself off as a crippled beggar, a blind man, a derelict, a leper, a ranting drunk, an out-of-work sailor, a cheap cut-throat, a drug pusher, a forger, a rake, a hired hand or a brothel-bouncer. I shelter under house-gutters, and get shooed away by servants; I spend hours concocting spurious prayers in churches whose cults no longer have any members. I sleep tucked away under bridges, where the mice take guided tours across my strange and ruined face.

I am living hidden away in some poor hovel up a narrow street; in the daytime I lie down under a window and can make out the shadows of passers-by as they move across the ceiling. Although everyone has an interest in capturing me, no one dares acknowledge what he suspects. I devour a few scraps I find discarded on the pavement and lap water from a tin plate. The street is so narrow that scarcely any light filters down to it. The shadows of the passers-by move silently across the ceiling: respectfully, as an accomplice or a threat. Early in the afternoon the light dies and the shadows fade. I hear footsteps for some time afterwards, becoming ever more hurried. Then they stop. After a while everything is silence, night is complete and only the natural gleam from the stone allows a glimpse of the outlines of the houses; it is then that I have the courage to get up, open the door and slip out into the street. In this street, facing the house where I have been hiding, stands another house, absolutely the same; it too has a half-open door, as if someone, hesitantly or wishing to go back inside at any moment, has just gone out. My own house is empty, for no one lives there except me, just as this other place which it looks on to is empty, stripped of its sole inhabitant. He lives in its main room, and his isolation is just as impossible as his presence. Stretched out on the pavement, or simply thrown there perhaps, lies an imperfect child. At first sight it does not appear as if the child's body is deficient, but anyone who looked more carefully would realise that this body is incapable of sustaining life. Everything appears to be normal, but nothing is properly fit for life. A creeping deformity affects every limb, the hands, feet and stomach, but not the face. And yet the child's face, when I see him as I do every night, seems aware, for all its silence, of the rest of his body and of its fate. His head lolls and his face, although it actually sees nothing, seems able to see. His gaze is intense yet lacks anything upon which to gaze; if it could bring hallucinations to life, they would be coherent and beautiful. I have no idea who cares for this child, nor how it has come to be deformed, a condition that existed before the child did and which has been made incarnate in him in a way that was not at all predictable. He seems to take no notice of my ghostly presence. He shows no fear of me, nor do I startle him. He shakes his hands weakly, displays signs of an unease that is not accompanied by any deep pain. Sometimes, he grows drowsy. In these moments I stare at his eyelids, which are quite unusually well defined and beautifully formed. I wonder all the time whether he will open them, and what sort of expression they will reveal. To what extent is he a participant in his own deformity? When he re-opens his eyes his gaze alights upon various objects, but he does not grasp what they are. I know that, one of these nights, his eyelids will close more heavily and even his questioning gaze will be definitively erased. I wonder whether I myself, who in the end am nothing more than this child's hallucination, will also become in that same moment — less defined.

A FEW HYPOTHESES CONCERNING MY PREVIOUS REINCARNATIONS

Although I am not thinking of implementing my companion's suggestions, but instead of keeping them in a state where they are perpetually deferred through haggling over their various terms, and skilfully, yet without any sense of satisfaction, misinterpreting them; and although I am not giving any especially favourable consideration to any specific form of death as being particularly appropriate to me, nevertheless I am embarking on a journey, along a corridor, then a garden path, in the course of which all these methods are displayed like ornaments, like a clock marking the time, or milestones: those who died by hanging themselves, those who slashed their throats, those who took poison and were overcome by a slow or precipitous torment the effects of which are visible in their wretched, haggard and translucent faces; skulls pierced by gunshots that often miss their exact target; the sound of shattering, or the scattered remains that cause one to look up in the expectation of seeing a window, bridge or tower; a rough image of a railway line with a body cut in two, its sex and history obliterated; a chaos of limbs destroyed by a self-inflicted immolation which simultaneously returns that person to the empyrean and down to the lowest depths. I move slowly through days coloured by the many different kinds of suicide, days that are sometimes so full that a froth of death spills over the edge and overflows; at other times only sensed as an exquisite but bitter scent; but I do not remember a single day in all my life when this gentle, anonymous counsellor, this dear mentor, did not walk just beside me, matching his pace to mine and never going before (which would be a discourteous act of cold domination), the sound of his footsteps always mingling with mine so that I understand him as an echo, a guardian angel, my consciousness, my double and shadow, my resonating steps and a memory. Yes, a memory: a loyal presence, stubborn but not arrogant, long-suffering but not monotonous, monotonous without being indiscreet, indiscreet without being arbitrary, arbitrary but never merely indiscriminate, indiscriminate but also stubborn, constant and patient, a presence that has always seemed appropriately my own; in fact, his suggestion of suicide (as I called it) does not pretend to be reasonable — it is, I would say, stubbornly tautological, and not without a touch of mockery, or a quite delicious irony, a play on words, a comment or a footnote so rambling as to be quite meaningless. Death approaches me, not at all welcomed, but referred to obliquely, in an act of Levantine generosity and solely because of the fact that I am alive. If it were philosophical advice being offered he would be able to dress up his abstraction as some kind of sententious apophthegm; for example:"That death is the rational aim of life, and suicide is the self-awareness of life made rational by death." But to utter such a proposition — well, then the shadow appears, the fake angel, a scratch or a mark that seems to crease itself into the shape of a smile or a joke; a sign that starkly shows me once again what makes his presence so special and dear to me: his amiable, unshakable companionship, long-standing ministrations and his being, that shadowy face composed from memory, a memory that I recognise — and not ungratefully — as being very very old.

   Just being born is enough to make one fully aware that every living thing carries within itself a project for death, that every life has its own specific and particular programme, and we can therefore conjecture that an inclination to suicide would adapt itself exactly to this programme; moreover, the will to commit suicide is only brought to an end by this death — and so becomes the being's consciousness and its conscience. Yet how approximate and inexact all of this is! How can this programme, or this project, ever give rise to the soft and dark verdure of spontaneity, and choose the actual manner of death? Would it not in fact tend towards the contrary? Namely: would the haphazard nature of death, or rather the stylistic vulgarity of a death that has been planned in detail, not take on a specific form, which would not therefore be suicide — with all its pretensions to choice of time, place, method and of meaning — but instead be a denial of that other, voluntary "death" which we all carry around with us, close beside us? It is thus a denial of the strategy of suicide, perhaps even its correction, as if that strategy was completely inadequate; in this case could it be that suicide — and here is a more ingenious interpretation — is a highly privileged form of death, completely self-contained, an exception to the "collective" programme and one that respects the individual's private agenda? But how — and why — could such a private programme be contrived when it runs so much against the grain? How can it be that the *unnaturalness* of suicide, concerning which the living seem to be completely convinced, gives way to this precious, spurious and excruciating specificity? I find myself faced with an apparent contradiction: that this kindly and angelic suicide I am talking about has co-existed within me for the whole of my life, like a memory that emerged at the moment I was born, free of any mundane causation of any kind whatsoever — failures in love, sorrows or other set-backs — but at the same time it has not become the natural and objective form of my life, because while this specificity allows me to suppose that suicide responds to a completely personal design, even so it still spills over the boundaries of my existence. Should I talk about suicide as an innate idea, as if it were a triangle or something that can be deduced by logic, or because this innate condition, this parallelogram of mortality, is uniquely mine, as if I possessed it by right on the basis of some privileged access to a universe of ideas, and that it is in this universe, among its numbers and its rhythms, that my ancient, immemorial suicide lies hidden?

Hence, I find myself involved in a suicide that is not a common form of existence, one that is not a consequence of my journey through life, nor yet a denial of the common form so much as a special variant of it. Can we agree that I have gained admission to a world of precise definitions and relevancies, and that I have done so through these same journeys? And given that the idea of suicide may be said to be congruent with that of triangles, will this condition not demonstrate that, since nothing is triangular except as a geometrical abstraction, in consequence no one is in fact able to kill themselves except in their imagination? Is the issue here not indeed the result of a definitive act of contemplation on my part which was granted, or imposed upon me, albeit certainly not during a state that was either natural or obviously specific? And, again: can it be true, perhaps, that I "remember" suicide in the same way as I remember triangles? My suicide may have been waiting in the place where I originated and, just like the triangle, could only leave that place by undertaking with me a sombre and fatal journey in which it would be pointless to distinguish the specific from the impersonal. But I am foolhardy enough to say I am sure of its character, which is relevant yet without cause; its perseverance, which is not of a dangerously obsessive nature; and finally the endless time during which this image has dwelt in my memory. Therefore, I return to a fact that is both a matter of opinion and a certainty: that my suicide is not imagined, invented, caused, inborn or unnaturally consistent, so much as *remembered.* When I put forward — as if in a purely intellectual game — this hypothesis, I realise that my intellect experiences some relief, as if this hypothesis thereby ceases to be unbearably strange. The unusual family likeness of this image is not a blood relationship but a resemblance to that other image, the triangle, and these images dwell together, in the form of a remembrance which embodies the exceptional nature of imagination and its significance, and which is barely veiled but still logical, not merely an intimation of a mood nor a susceptibility to melancholy or inner sorrow, but rather something similar to a chess move, a solution to a problem I am not yet aware of, while being secretly and unquestionably linked to it, and both obscured and illuminated by the condition of remembrance. In short, the deep-seated feeling I have that I might owe my birth itself to suicide, and that this may have been what fathered me. For this hypothesis has a singularly calming effect, as if I had noticed a sound — forgotten but not completely erased from memory — such as the rasp of a hinge being forced open, something as familiar as it once was: I recognise the faint, subtle smell of the dwelling of some scrupulous person; various noises from the street, or voices to which I dare attach no words or names; in point of fact here, the fantasy of remembrance is augmented by the fantasy of return, and both are more relevant than consolatory; I dare not linger over this exercise, considering whether more facts may emerge for further examination, in order to discover whether I am allowed to welcome this ancient and reasonable companion: my inclination towards suicide. And when I say I am "reminded" of a suicide that is my own, this can only mean that I have already killed myself. Let us say, therefore, that I have ended a life with an intentional death; with this act I have frozen it, sealed and distinguished it; and in this way I found my life again, today; as if I had started off again from where another life had finished; and therefore it is registered as my suicide, and forwarded, so to speak, with all the documents and records pertaining to my previous life but in the style that would typically be associated with a certificate of achievement. So it becomes clear now how I can know that this suicide is a recollection — and thus may instil in me some sort of motivation — which somehow goes beyond the borders of my conscious life; but more, that the suicide of my former life was sent to me as both a solution and a problem. Let us accept then (and not without some amusement) that I have killed myself in a former life and have begun my life again with this problem. If I perceive suicide as a "recollection", a problem, that must mean that in my former existence it did not bring about the resolution that was longed for, but has simply confirmed the problem with implacable ruthlessness by placing me in a condition of perpetual suicide, as if the challenge had to be restored to me intact, so that I might choose between suicide as a gesture or suicide as a problem. If, in the life preceding, the suicide treated as a gesture passed this propensity on to me intact, does that mean perhaps that I should treat it, in my current life, as a problem?

I have said that a suicide in a former existence failed to bring about a resolution, and was therefore an inadequate solution to a pre-existing problem. Instead, this suicide which, although acted upon, fell short of what was needed, has been added to the problem, and thereby constitutes a new problem, one that is more difficult and harsh, even psychotic. It is therefore no longer a problem which may be clarified by intellectual inquiry or by pure thought, but one which is already tainted by an uncomfortably imprecise solution; consequently it will not be enough to resolve the imprecise solution, for it is not simply an error but has become a part of the problem itself. If this complicates the task that now faces me it does at least have a beneficial aspect in that, along with the error, it passes on to me this other problem which has become inextricably bound up with it, which preceded it and which until now was unknown to me.

The argument is now more complex, but its relevance has become more precise and my initial feeling of calm has given way to a kind of exhilaration. In summary, I took my life in response to a problem which was not resolved by that action; or which I was hoping, by the same token, to leave unresolved; or to force it upon others, as a form of revenge, accusation or denunciation; or to extract from them an extreme act of piety. Now, I cannot ask myself directly what this unresolved and implacable problem might be; but because I have supposed that it was compounded by suicide, concerning which I now admit to having a clear recollection, I have tried to retrace its outlines within that suicide. The theme of suicide has therefore been growing in importance, becoming persistent, rhythmic, impetuous, insinuating, scornful and allusive, abating and flaring up again within the context of a discussion, a dialogue with a supreme and pre-existent shadow; a dialogue at times accusatory, defensive, sarcastic, querulous, crafty, adversarial, highly rhetorical, persuasive to the point of being corrupt, insidious or disloyal. Sometimes I tried to make it my accomplice, by declaring a detailed and pedantic description of my daily sorrows. I displayed my wounds with the punctilious bravura of a beggar. And it always came to my aid, like some sort of emotional counsellor, this friendly shadow of suicide. Thereafter, suicide took part in a discussion with a different, threatening shadow, which I will call "deity".

This entails the recognition of a nature, or rather an imagination, that inclines towards the religious. In fact, private misfortunes, unhappiness and illness have never fed the suicide's project, so that it must find its means of nourishment elsewhere. I have never thought that my suicide had anything to do with being carried away by passion; my suicide has always had an institutional character. Now, there is no question that those with a religious imagination are led to meditating upon, and dealing with death, their own and that of others, so it would not be rash to suppose that my problem, my error, concerns precisely how death is to be interpreted.

A religious imagination, the meaning of death, a failed suicide that generates a further problem; such complexities lead me to believe that this was not a matter of a private error, but an institutional one: a religious error. Only extremely specific circumstances could justify an outcome so catastrophic and at the same time so packed with allusion. My hypothesis is that I was a priest when I killed myself. Here then is a new consolatory impulse, for this seems to indicate that my preceding life assigned to me, in this dialogue with a deity, not only suicide as a rhetorical figure but also my being related, in some way, to the figure of a priest. I feel it is pointless to investigate, either then or now, what kind of priest.

So: a priest committed suicide and thereby perpetrated a theological error; or he was overwhelmed by some problem which I cannot consider to be private. My hypothesis is that the two conditions are both true in part, and are inextricably bound up with each other. Suicide may present itself as an extreme submission to some theological conformity that could not be tolerated in daily life; or it may have borne testimony to the shocked recognition of a falsely theological contradiction, which in reality was a contradiction of the flesh.

But if it is true that my suicide does not find nourishment in passionate adventures, and if it is true that this suicide which I am now "living" is exactly what was passed on to me by my former life, then I am unable to imagine that this priest's suicide can have been motivated only by sexual passion, although it seems likely that the affair may have had a certain romantic element — an abstract one perhaps. We may imagine that this suicide also involved some kind of struggle with a deity — perhaps the deity of that very religion of which I was then a priest — and therefore its character was both theological and emotional. For a priest to kill himself seems a particularly dramatic act, and precisely for that reason we must assume that this gesture includes an intolerable theological element. Suicide is not, however, necessarily an irreligious or subversively blasphemous act. There is, indeed, a specific kind of suicide which religion has dignified by a supreme designation: namely, martyrdom. For those stimulated by the subject of suicide, religion provides this pious version. Even so, I must conclude that the suicide I committed as a priest was not done out of piety, although that does not necessarily mean that it was impious. I may have committed suicide because I had misinterpreted the terms of the problem, or alternatively because I was under the delusion that I was conferring a martyrdom upon myself, in order, for example, to free someone who was attached to me by the anguish of a passionate relationship; here is a suicide that also demonstrates a theological failing, a challenge, or even a vague religious proposition; and from this arises the problem with which I live on a daily basis, and which I fear is insoluble.

Of late, this half-fantastic and half-mythological formulation has greatly pleased me and even furnished me with a sense of dignity, something that is certainly based on reasoning which I realise is false, but which I would not know how to secure otherwise. In fact, through being implicated in an argument — even a weak argument — with the deity, who is linked to death by the professional compulsion of collectors, the priest himself is violent in a special way. I would venture to say that, theologically speaking, the priest is a murderer, in so far as his position puts him on the side of death — or, more precisely, on the side of the one who kills. But let us surmise that even though he may be on the side of death, and takes on the guise of a killer, one does not often find a priest who makes his ability to kill the foundation of his theology. So he is a priest, certainly, but one incapable of pitting himself against this vast, contradictory and disastrous capacity for death, for participating in death, and making it happen. The reality is that the ability to kill, like that of accomplishing certain modest miracles, is something we all have in common, but which becomes catastrophic when it is not linked to the possibility of being situated within a theological framework. For hatred is unavoidable, and unless it is a sacrament it cannot be anything *other* than catastrophic. Now, if hatred cannot be given the same meaning as death, which would be the inclination of a killer, it does at least create havoc in the life of the person who hates. If I examine my own life, I feel certain that I have been both a priest and a victim of suicide, in circumstances that seem to be connected with the power to foresee things, but also with a sense of being overwhelmed by a fearful hatred, a hatred with no purpose at all, just the pure and simple craving to destroy others. As with suicide — and this fact is what convinces me of the soundness of my argument — such a hatred has no basis in reality; I forget what offended me, my annoyance is short-lived; I do not dislike the friend who cheated me, but loathe beyond all reason the man who has done me no harm. I would not kill an enemy, but I have dallied with destroying people whom I knew very well to be innocent. I am the wiliest of diplomats in the art of convincing the innocent that it is in the nature of justice that I persecute them with a special hatred which cannot be appeased.

Therefore, whether I am corroborating or dreaming up a pre-birth suicide, so to speak, if I situate the figure of a priest in the same place, if I discover at last that there is a hatred which cannot be situated in theology, perhaps then I will be allowed a further hypothesis, namely that this hatred does not belong originally to the priest, but to the protagonist of an existence before this, and that the hatred in question was a problem deriving from this former existence, to which, in the life that followed, the priest had vainly tried to find a resolution. If I re-examine the hatred which in my life merges with the theme of suicide, I recognise it as something that is only marginally religious; consequently, let us imagine it is associated with the emotions, for the passions may conceal just such an impersonal, imprecise and dramatically anonymous motif. But, if it is the case that this association with hatred extends to me from two lives previous, then I must assume that I have killed in pursuit of a hatred of a very powerful nature. No crime is easier to unmask than a crime of passion, which necessarily entails a certain derangement and an instantly satiated yearning for death. Frequently, the murderer himself boasts of his crime, and becomes so arrogant that he offers himself up to the judgement of his fellow men — a sign that the passionate man is on the side of death, and in that respect is akin to the priest, but only as regards his own death and the death of the object of his passion. In this case, therefore, I would have been apprehended or discovered. It is quite possible that I was condemned to death. I may also have committed a murder and had my life taken from me: but I do not think that this was the case. In fact, if that did take place, the subsequent suicide of the priest would not constitute, in my understanding, a specific error in this new way of posing the problem, but merely a simple reiteration, and would thus be incompatible with its original formulation as it had been articulated in relation to the existence of the priest.

Now, I wish to make one additional point. My initial assumptions amounted to: priest, suicide, hatred; however, I also have another tenuous notion, one that is scarcely even sketched in, that I was executed, and have the memory of a death, some sort of public death, which was enjoyed in good conscience by others. I would like, then, to insist on this final proposition: if I have been killed by "everyone", it is not unreasonable to suppose that in my case there are three possible ways for me to be reborn like "everyone", yet still hold on to my hatred, but in a socially acceptable and justifiable form: as a soldier, executioner or politician. Otherwise I might be born the overseer of an absolute hatred on behalf of someone who had hated me absolutely, and in this case I might rediscover the unique and all-consuming calling that is rebellion; or again as the interpreter of a collective hatred, with the ability to translate the executioner's destiny according to theological criteria.

In my opinion, it is the last two of these hypotheses, in that exact sequence, which are most valid.

This then reveals a new type of hatred and of the person who hates, which through the application of simple dialectics I would situate between hatred-passionate and hatred-theological, and which I will call hatred-generic. To differentiate from the previous forms of hatred, this hatred is not embodied in relationships between people and neither does the person who hates hate everyone indiscriminately. It is the fact of being born among his fellow men that he cannot abide. If, in this former life — now the fourth distant from my present life — men similar to me, my "fellows", have handed me over to the executioner's justice, then a wrong has come down to me that cannot be made right. Quite clearly, in the life in which I committed murder I could not deny that I deserved to die; but I was not able to accept a death that was legally sanctioned, especially since it defined fellowship in a certain way. The hatred that destroyed me was repugnant precisely because it was "just" and a social matter of companionship and practicality; because it masqueraded as not being hatred. If this new incarnation had followed the priest's, the eventual problem would never have arisen. I assume, therefore, that the figure of the rebel must have inserted itself, owing to the fact that he is one who hates in the generic mode because he is the object of a hatred-generic which he finds insupportable. And not only this: having, in a fit of passion, killed, I then actively engaged myself in this machinery that was in the service of hatred; I had stirred up a dynamic of hatred for which my death had not been able to provide protection, but which instead transferred itself to the life that succeeded it, into which it intruded with greater rapidity. I suppose I had developed further, in becoming an assassin, but in an impersonal way; and that in the end I was killed, but not executed. It is vital in this instance that my death was not the work of collective justice, and that the good conscience of the social fraternity was not implicated; rather that it was a death that was to some degree random, a brush with other killers, which combined in equal proportion both detached and focused violence. If he or they who killed me were unaware either of who I was or why I should be killed, then they in turn were collaborating to create a new form of hatred and of death, more abstract than generic, not so much specific as impersonal.

Having spurned the death delivered by justice, having accepted death by affray whilst being fully aware that it was inadequate, it only remained for me to face the whole problem of this new form of hatred, and its associated death, both active and passive: the problem of the priest's incarnation. It is probable that initially I was deluded into thinking that with this supposition I had settled all the preceding problems. Unfortunately my theological awareness was not very profound.

This optimistic hypothesis — which I suppose took its inspiration from my experience as a priest — touched on the following topics: that legal and brotherly hatred were brought to an end; the executioner took on a cosmic role; hatred-fortuitous was redeemed by hatred-comprehensive but not hatred-generic throughout the world by the desire to avoid being interpreted by theology, by way of its reluctance to progress from Existence to Being. But there was — though it was completely relevant — a faint touch of the sophist's arrogance in this interpretation. The facts of the case are these: in the first of my hypothesised existences I hated with a hatred so vehement that it bordered on murder; this hatred, I now understand, survived intact, and was invulnerable to theological transformation; it was a completely specific hatred, an ingenious malformation which I had neither forgotten nor remembered. It would have been easy to bring about the transformation of this hatred of myself as an assassin — because it was already impersonal, and thus covertly philosophical, even if only in a weak and illiterate manner — except that the other hatred belonged to a truly academic discipline, the art of killing one specific individual.

I presume this individual was a woman. I cannot possibly know anything about her, but I can, yet again, form a few hypotheses: for example, that within the programme of her life, a certain kind of death was expected for her; that her programme had been different and that my killing had changed it, but not the dynamic that was foreshadowed by its design; finally, that she had launched her own individual attack upon the programme that included her normal death, with a violent premeditated death; to sum up, it was a suicide at the hands of a third party: me as a priest.

This argument, now that I have set it down, seems quite remarkably illuminating. The fact is, if the woman had been killed in conformity with her planned trajectory, I would not have committed a theological crime, and so I as priest would in effect have corrected the original imprecision; in some respects I would have planned and committed the crime. My death, in a case of this nature, having its origins in her legitimate death, would not have required the complex rectification that was demonstrated primarily by the fact of a priest's suicide.

But if, through the act of killing, I had destroyed this design, I must then infer that I had completely undermined the dynamics of death, and had stirred up a controversy which was bound to be presented again, as far as was possible, in a new existence, but with all its original elements changed and quite differently combined. Although very much obscured, her image would be able to intermingle with the image of death during a conflict in her subsequent existence: not, to be precise, as a direct cause, but as a character, a witness, whereby she herself was killed in the struggle perhaps (and this is a hypothesis I find most attractive), and killed by my hand to prevent her from falling into the violating hands of other killers. I am really delighted to present this final hypothesis for it introduces with unerring relevance the final confrontation, between the priest and the woman herself. Consider this: if I as a priest had met this same woman, if the same throat, the same forehead, had been presented to me, as the focus of my hatred, then I can well imagine that I, as a priest and agent of an unnamed hatred, refusing to repeat that forgotten but still-present act, and, in order to save her, killed myself. Although such an act would not have resolved the theological problem of hatred, at least I would have confronted it with a daringly theological suicide.

But let us imagine that the woman — who came to an agreement with me, she in her most persistent form and I in the guise of a priest — was set in each of these instances on destroying her own programme for death; that she put herself forward as a victim, let us say, or more precisely, as a suicide; an act of suicide that did not originate in a choice made out of sentiment, but for theological reasons; that, in the end, this concept was, for her, innate — as has been supposed to have been the case for me as the man of passion, criminal and then priest — and that it came to her along undiscovered pathways. Here then is the denouement! Having fallen into the obscure reaches of an intrigue that was only obliquely emotional in its oldest existence; being driven on by this error to a ferocious hatred, but not without suspecting an emotional element in her new and violent death; then, this fatal dialogue moves on to a meticulous discovery of the impersonal implications of the situation; the priest makes no distinction between the three stages of hatred, or between a death that is sought and a death that is suffered; and although the priest is able to escape the woman's determination to be murdered, it is possible to evade that death only by interposing himself between his own self and the woman; so that, thereby, a higher, but not definitive level is reached, in relation to the death that preceded this one.

And the woman? We cannot deny that she handles the Man of Passion, the Criminal and Priest, all of them, in the same way, as a weapon. There is then a particular problem, the problem of the woman.

If she succeeded in using me as a weapon it is because in the first instance she put herself forward as a direct target; the second time, as an incidental victim, or, if my speculation is not ungrounded, a victim of love; but the third time she fell hopelessly short of her objective, because the incarnation as a priest established an absolute divide between personal and theological hatred. Although this resolution was somewhat vague, the outline of the problem was entirely relevant. Therefore the woman's repeated attempts at finding death are not only related to her personal history, but also form a part of the history of the problem itself, about which, as we have seen, the priest was mistaken, though only partially. As a priest, I have directly understood this woman as exemplifying a particular theological problem; I also know that by making myself a priest, I committed myself to bringing the problem to a resolution; but that, simultaneously, the status of priest was bound to heighten the tension between personal and theological hatred; and that this pressure was used by the woman as a particular weapon; without success, however, and even disastrously so. Becoming a priest meant that I was committed to recognising the passionate hatred that is present within theology, and thus the murderer within the executioner, with the result that I acquired a hatred which allowed me to kill the entire world, and along with the world, to kill myself, but not, notably, to kill a single one of its overall population. This hatred, however, this archaic and irreducible hatred, had been restored to me but in a different guise: no longer associated with passion, alien to violence, it was nevertheless incapable of becoming theology. The challenge of the woman who wished to be killed was not acted upon; but the hatred appeared in various forms, nameless and ambiguous, disguised and inexhaustible; and I, the priest, killed myself.

It is not beyond possibility that I might actually have already met this very woman, and the challenge, which I have neither overcome nor yielded to, is still before me, and is unfinished. I am now able to gather up in my hands the threads of my various incarnations in their original form, as problems; an ecclesiastical response, in some respects, though tied to no faith. In what form can I acquire that theological hatred within which all other hatreds are to be found? Further puzzling reincarnations lie in wait for me, perhaps, and the light of this discovery — which now makes my heart ache, and dazzles me — will seem to me only a faint and peripheral illumination; but to my "I" of the coming century, I have nothing better to offer.

IGNOMINY

One gets the feeling that, in large measure, it may come down to a question of skill; although it is impossible to tell what kind of skill may be involved, knitting a crack together, perhaps, or learning how to distinguish the fault-line where something has fractured? In any case this place especially seems riven with fissures, although it is not possible to tell whether they lead anywhere. Perhaps what is required, once again, is for we dead to make a show of being "worthy", but if that's the case, it is not clear what kind of worthiness is meant, and how it might be verified. Besides, it does not seem possible, given the state I am in, that there is any reason to pose the question of dignity, or whether I myself share in this worthiness. It is strange that — even though, by definition, I have no body, and therefore occupy no position in space — what seems to make the question of skill pointless is the unreasonable and completely useless horizontal position I have assumed, as imprinted on me by death at the time when I still had a body; I resemble a thread, with my head facing backwards in relation to the position in which my body would have lain, all of which combined leaving me with no sense of direction. Now, in this state of being dead — the final moment and the one closest to my state of being alive — I think of myself, although I have no substance, as being uniformly and utterly flat, capable of advancing using my forearms and my feet which are at the same height as my head, just like a thread trying to insert itself into the eye of a needle, an unseeing thread, or, better still, a thread which because of some slub in the material, or resulting from chastisement (if a thread can be chastised), has become twisted about so that it can only look backwards; a thread that strives with its feet, to pass through a needle's eye, yet which not only does not know its position, but also does not know if it even exists, and although it is sure that there must be a needle's eye here in this space, it does not have, I do not have, any idea whether it is possible to catch sight of it and so slip through; furthermore, as I was saying, these cracks, or rips — which in some respects are quite like cracks that I seem to recognise and to have passed through, if to no effect — and these rings of scribbling which have of their own accord wrapped themselves around my body, have given me a false sensation of motion, and advancement.

I happened to mention the word "body" again there, but I know, just as anyone knows who ends up in this place, that there are no bodies here, not just mine, but no bodies at all, categorically so, and that this non-body is at the same time not, in any circumstance whatsoever, a place or a space. And yet — and yet — I was thinking and talking about myself as if I did indeed have a shape, or an outline, but yes, with no shoes of course, even if they had put them on the body; without a jacket, no trousers and no tie, not even a somewhat old-fashioned tie that had been chosen perhaps because it had been a particular favourite, or which was appropriate to my state of being dead. Of course, the absence of shoes is entirely obvious, but that my feet should also be missing is deeply disturbing. I am making too much of it perhaps, but it really is rather troubling, especially if, as I say, I have to use — what else could I use? — little toes, big toes, to test for this needle's eye, using a toe which does not exist to locate a hole, and something that would not exist even if this place was a place. Let us see then: I could consider myself as the hole; let us imagine that there is a world, that I am not a part that has been cut out of it but rather whatever remains behind after something else has been cut away, something that resembles a void and which has not come about from natural causes, but as the result of problems to do with disease, denial or sin. Should something fill this space which resulted from something being cut away, that thing would be in a state of violation, a failing so objective that it could not by its very nature occur, since at this level there is a very real dread of committing such a transgression, that is, of inhabiting a void that is so defined and so complete; if that void itself had an outline, it would be the outline of a corpse; although I myself am not a corpse in any respect, nor have I ever been a corpse because no one can be a corpse, although some manage — it's a matter of skill, or perhaps a means of self-protection — to assume the appearance of a corpse.

Earlier on I mentioned the tie, and there is perhaps nothing that distresses me more than this, that I am unable to remember anything at all about that tie, that useless object which was supposed to signify my worth, my respectability. It is strange that a dead person is not allowed to remember his tie, even though he can remember his shoes, his suit, some tiny detail of the funeral parlour, some little thing the mourners left behind, like the spare change that is no longer legal tender that one comes across discarded in a drawer. Ties are definitely associated with some deeper denial, although in this respect not so much a punishment for vanity — for what is the point of punishing a strip of emptiness? — as an absolute "no" to the possibility of giving them any respect. I have no idea whether I was thin or fat; but I imagine I was slim, for what reason I simply do not know since I do not even remember, and nor does it interest me, how my death came about. A lengthy illness, perhaps, a vicious assault, a killing that came out of the blue or an act of contrived violence — while the idea of expulsion is common to all forms of death, it is only murder that really exists, or so it seems to me. Yet perhaps I am lying or deceiving myself when I insist that the manner of my death is a matter of indifference to me; the fact that I have my being here, even if I do not exist here, and that I am seeking the eye of the needle, all of this must be linked to the process that sealed my own expulsion from that other place.

Let us suppose that I arrived here by way of a violent death, either at my own hand or someone else's. If it was by my own hand, it is reasonable to suppose that I did not wish to annihilate myself (something which seems to be impossible), so much as to go into hiding; and since there is no more extensive, nor comfortable place to hide in than this, I have hidden myself away here, quite sure that I would not be recognised, with my face all drawn and unreadable, crouched in the centre of the sphere of the deepest shadows, in my artful way, where no human hand can reach me and where I am not obliged to interpret any voices, screams, pronouncements or messages. But is it always the case that those who hide do not wish to be found? Some of them may perhaps be seeking to set up a situation that is so intimidating that only the person they have in mind — strangely enough — would be able to track them down, a filter that blocks out everyone, except — who? Let us say someone who may have a taste for darkness and the emptiness of place. But if such a person should fail to arrive, what would it mean then? That no one cares about this hiding place or about whoever has hidden away here, and that this pointless winking, this mawkish, flirtatious and provocative posturing from within the shroud of non-existence appears only to be a sort of indiscretion. In that case, what will the person in hiding do? Without question he will fall into a kind of abjection and will simply stop moving, making only slight gestures, and even those politely and not at all assertively; if no one (let alone the one he had in mind) comes forward, he will be overcome by a strange ennui, and will begin to tear off those strips of stuff that no one else will remove in order to see what sort of face this nothing might have who is crouched here below, and then hopefully

seek the needle on his own account and thus attempt to escape his hiding place…
But maybe the person who was hiding had put himself into a false situation, or
lacked the necessary skills, or was overrated, or a nuisance, and even if he had
aspirations, how could he not be aware of this? In such a situation any skills he
might have had would fall away, and this fellow will stumble, caught up in dreams
of fantastical and pointless strategies, before drifting into failure yet again and
understanding that he lacks the ability of ever finding the eye of the needle, and
that there is little hope that someone will just lend him a hand — because he is
hidden, and will stay hidden, and his absence will arouse no interest, astonishment
or disquiet. And if one day, not by any design but simply by chance, he should
happen across a needle, it is entirely possible that the shock of that event, the
resurgence of the "here", together with voices and hands, would drive him to hide
himself away again, for he does not know how to do anything else.

If my death by violence was at someone else's hand, I should provide a specific
example: namely death at the hands of a murderer *ad personam* who wished me
dead because of some wrong I had committed, or because he wanted to divest me
of a form that resembled my own, or simply because I was obnoxious. If I was sent
to my doom by a single hand, then I have no reason to question the fundamental
integrity of that judgement, for the jury was so reduced, and so set upon its
verdict — that such a person should no longer be permitted to live — and
therefore I must hypothesise that the reason for my death was evidently my
fundamental worthlessness, something that cannot be explained let alone put
right, and which implies that the universe was made this way to include both me
and my executioner. In such a case I would have been expelled, banished from the
place of the "here" and summarily — even if impartially — cast into this other
place of the "not here". Now, as happens with anyone who has been convicted of
a crime, it is not beyond the bounds of possibility that I would drag my heels a

little, because, even if I do not question the justice of the sentence, I nevertheless remain convinced that one particular line of my defence should have been allowed — a common and irritating assertiveness on my part when the whole world has witnessed my expulsion and has certainly gone along with it. Even so it is perfectly possible that I can be both convinced and annoyed, and for that reason seek the needle's eye, in the same way that a loose woman might, or some petty thief caught in the act of a shameful and tawdry theft but who still tries to dream up a defence, even if it is a contentious piece of reasoning — in short, I "play the victim", which is exactly the last thing a murdered person would do, and I am seeking the needle's eye exactly for that very reason, because I want to speak of it as mine, and because I want the last word — a childish attitude when all the words have already been spoken, and as for all the reasons I could come up with, who would find them interesting? But what seems strange to me is that we always try to plead our case in the exact same place where we are convicted, tried and found wanting, whereas instead we might seek out a situation in which all this would be of no consequence, or equally seek to discover a place where public opinion is indifferent to those who have been murdered: in short, to go somewhere else, whatever that means.

However, the situation could be that I was in fact killed in some insignificant fashion, for instance, when I was crossing a road or because I had a bent nose; in such a case I may have died at an early age, or anyway younger than usual, and perhaps not on my own; hence I would have been expelled in a manner that was anonymous, collective, perfunctory and bureaucratic. A death of this kind is completely routine, and nothing more. Murdering a man in this way does not mean that he is especially worthless, it means only that he is ill mannered and tainted with a certain degree of worthlessness, an unhealthy and unpleasant condition which persists everywhere since simply being alive is to foul oneself. A typical symptom of life is often present in such people, namely death, and in particular a voluntary death, although it is not so much this symptom that kills them, but the diagnosis itself; or, rather, the diagnosis becomes the symptom that kills their understanding that they are dead. In all of this there is a revelation of violence that cannot be understood except as the dread, fateful clarity which the sick man knows all too well when, while idly leafing through a medical dictionary, he finds his own case described in great detail, perhaps even that he is named personally, and the final prognosis set out with terrifying precision.

Those who have died in this manner are scattered about in the "not here"; having no need for space they find themselves at such a distance from one another that there is no way they can be compared, and accordingly they each acquire a kind of spurious dignity that is more treacherous and humiliating than any kind of derision, rather a derision to which there is no adequate reply — for who is able to challenge anyone else in the "here"? And indeed would we really want to challenge their condition, when I suspect we rather enjoy this unfortunate and heartbreaking joke? The feeling of the dead person in this situation is that everything has happened in too disorganised a manner — disastrous and undignified too, because he was so bound up in the process; but, naturally, he is lying to himself, for it cannot be ignored that it was precisely this way of killing he had resorted to, so that in dealing with him a general air of worthlessness becomes apparent, an infection of worthlessness which prevents him from making a detailed inventory of his own particular revolting indecency — if that is not (given the circumstances) too strong a way of expressing myself. But in the end this foolish dead man — and I could be one of them myself — seeks the eye of the needle because he tells himself that in other circumstances things could have turned out differently, it seems to him that his death "doesn't count" and he would like a second go, which he will be denied of course, or rather no one will take any notice of his request — bureaucracy everywhere is able to solve such matters by procrastination — and eventually the dead man forgets how he came to be this way, and then of being in such a condition, and ultimately stops bothering, for who cares about a few cursory coincidental whimpers heard centuries apart, especially here, in this place where there are no ears?

Since I am not short of time, I want to consider a more sophisticated example: someone has tried to murder me, and succeeded in wounding me, but I survived, the perpetrator repented but in the end I died as a result of my wounds. It is a particularly unpleasant case, since this death, administered one step at a time, cannot do anything but place me in a false position, one that is defensive and marked by self-justification, and which is abetted in this instance by the murderer's repentance, which provides a semblance of support for my disapproval. Sometimes the killer in such cases is overtaken by remorse, which is generally understood as the regret of an upright conscience being swept aside by a summary and omnipresent malaise — but which I think should actually be seen as a symptom, a sign of universal discontent with the killer's incompetence, perhaps enabled by chance but in the event found wanting, when all along it was completely up to him to manage his self-awareness of the worthlessness of being alive.

In such a case the dogged fury of the dead man may easily resort to the awkward business of self-justification, often exacerbated by the sophistry of others; the dead man hears someone calling him from the other side of the needle's eye, which is both a stressful and an undignified situation, and moreover something much to be pitied.

Because illness continues to be the most common cause of death, I will hypothesise that I died that way myself; how can there be any doubt that all the dead have not wondered that at a certain point in their existence, whether there was — so to speak — a mistake along the route, a sign that turned out to be misleading, and which directed them towards catastrophe, even though the road was quite straight, clear and wide? Why did we choose, through what trick of the senses or tangled confusion of information were we, all spattered with mud, led to pitch and plunge down this by-way, which with every yard lost the appearance of a road and turned out to be nothing more than a dirt-track? How was it possible for us to forego that huge abundance of illumination, burdensome though it might have been, in order to take refuge among these unthreatening shadows, in an originary absence of light? A mistake was made, certainly, but the mistake did not just happen — was it stitched into our flesh right from the start, was this track always to be our principal thoroughfare, and what light could our eyes have tolerated? When have we ever known how to distinguish a single voice amidst the clamour of so many others? How is it that we dare to believe ourselves to be the victims of a particular injustice, or of an error that could be made good, at the precise moment when we want to put ourselves forward again for a new journey, like a ball in a game of pinball? Why do our hypothetical feet strive for the eye of the needle? Or is the needle's eye a myth too perhaps?

Quite possibly nothing would be more humiliating than this: that the eye was not in fact a myth. Whatever the pretext, I try, as one who is dead, to find the right way through: I am sure of my ability to clarify matters, to set them straight, bring about my pardon, find the correct road, explain everything and no longer find myself on the wrong track. It is conceivable, certainly, that our confused hopes, this ignominy of being alive and of being dead, is what forces us to dream up these tiresome deceptions — but does our shame not have its accomplices? Is it in fact possible that we find ignominy so pleasant and so enjoyable that it incites the one who visits ignominy upon us to make it eternal? And that, although the quest we pursue with our feet for the eye is ungainly and absurd, could there be anything more ridiculous than the rediscovery of that eye? Oh, we all know who could pass through the eye of the needle without ignominy — yes, it is the murderer — but which one of us is actually a murderer ?

It may be that getting agitated harms the dead, or makes void their void. Certainly, if I was a murderer — if one of us were the murderer, if among we dead someone began to assemble the character, the profession (am I framing this precisely enough?) of the murderer, all of this could recover, if not sentience, then dignity, dignity at least. But what then? Would one of us alone be sufficient to constitute the character of the murderer, or can we succeed only if we all act together? Can we, the dead, learn in unison, by thus sticking together, how to delineate a fictitious and yet real, and truly homicidal murderer... one who would not have before his eyes *the eye*, who would not be permitted to pass through it without explaining anything to anybody, and thus would be unable to return, that is we dead would be unable to return, except as this single murderer, a murderer who intends to murder no one but himself?

All that sounds extremely ambitious. For a dead man who is denied even the embellishment of a tie is it not a capricious piece of arrogance to wish to absent oneself from ignominy, the habitual ignominy of the dead? Look — I'm laughing.

AN IMPOSSIBLE LOVE

oble Princess,

You must forgive me, I beg you, if maintaining my deeds in step with an audacious dream requires that I venture to advance myself as far as the periphery of your gaze, and perhaps it will surprise you to receive this letter as much as it surprises me to send it. My own dear Marcellus, a versatile and theoretical fellow, having recently returned from his German university so famous for its metaphysical games of the mind, has conjured up for me a portable verbal catapult, by means of which I dare to sling, through the darkness of space, this missile of veneration, this steed of rhetoric ridden by a messenger who is more incoherent than eloquent, the head of a comet whose dishevelled and tawny locks etch a design in flames upon the shadowy emptiness and illuminate an initial letter on the bellies of the clouds.

Why do I write to you? Because I am fantastical and melancholy, and I suppose you melancholy and gentle too. Because I seek wild and whirling acts, false new years and artificial epiphanies; because by now, upon our platform[1] carved from the shadows, our gestures and poses of eternal death are all eaten away by worms, and gradually decay, because with each of Ophelia's deaths, with each death of mine, with every disinterment of Yorick,[2] the flat, stale universe casts over us the shadow of its dishonest resentment. We know as much. In a short while the shadows will scroll over us, wiping our escutcheon from the gates of heaven. Yet before that should come to pass — and all that remains of the degenerate court of Denmark is the memory of a solecism, or a grim lesson set down in some codex and abandoned in the empty library of the stars — I dare to attempt this calculatedly blasphemous act, both to challenge and to solicit this consummation devoutly to be wished,[3] and artfully procured, but also to provoke the rough hand of the gods; to challenge, like some impertinent street urchin, that celestial bully who pins us to the wall with his hairy, ring-haloed hand; and to entangle and blunt our rapier in the ostentation of his purple cloak, so that from this somewhat clumsy thrust there should arise quips and irreverent jibes expressed with pointed sarcasm which will at last ensure that we may meet to cross swords in an alley that lies between Hell and the empyrean, and thereby bring to an end, together with this confused and tedious soliloquy, the burden of dying every day amidst this hackneyed celebration of elegant deaths and impossible loves.

Princess, there is a graciousness about you, and melancholy sufficient to understand what I write; do not condemn me, but rather judge me as one afflicted by the sickness of this perfectly imperfect existence, and desirous of a conclusion that is more conclusive, a death that might provoke other deaths or offer a subversive aside not envisaged by the script with which to break in upon some private dialogue, as with the man who, once the adulterous queen has been slain, whispers this with a twitch of his lecherous wrinkles, "I'll visit you this evening, at seven."[4]

Your devoted Hamlet kisses your hand. I here enclose the instructions for the manufacture of the verbal catapult, calibrated so as to enable you to reply with ease, if so you should desire; as ardently I hope.

Noble Prince,

You may easily imagine with what astonishment I received your message — I who am confined here in this paradise of Colombelles.[5] But I do not venture to reprove you for your audacity, for so heavy is the lifeless languor endured here among these brocades, and so thickly are the *faux* crimsons of these heraldic escutcheons covered with shadows, that one lives in an ambience crowded with whispers, but quite deprived of lips to utter them, so that it happens sometimes that even a women such as I — cautious, and not displeased by orderly torments — longs for an awkward gesture, a discourteous cry, some protestation of extravagant grief. And perhaps your message, to which I have chosen to reply as a diversion, or rather because of the mild disapproval it arouses in me, falls into this category. Certainly it reveals a mind overthrown; but not ignobly so.[6] Throughout this constricted space, which I have called paradise, there clings the perpetual odour of moths, dust in the air and the taint of decaying velvets, a vegetal agony; in truth, this paradise is dying. And while my unfortunate husband is dying too, and the Duke of Nemours[7] wearily, reluctantly, moves on to other loves — persuaded by the unhappy state of his body and the immature disorder of his soul — while I undertake laboured conversations with the man to whom I am legally bound, I hear a scraping, the scratching of a cat, of claws on silk; I am the only one perhaps who is aware of this. But certainly there are others, the courtiers with their blighted, noble skin, who recognise that our paradise is in agony. They try not to frighten me; they feign a courtly calm, these poor players; but already they forget their lines and fluff their entrances, not, however, through any loss of memory — their professional competence is beyond all doubt — but because a deferential terror leads them astray and distracts them. Two days ago my husband died, and almost two hours early; the Duke of Nemours wrote me a delightful little note, with three spelling mistakes; the Duke of Guise was on the point of coming to blows with my husband… They are all boys about to die; they think I would not notice their fear and they wish to die as men; what could be more childish? I feel sorry for them, with all the maternal concern of a barren mother. My fear is that I would be the only one not to know fear, because I live in a state of perpetual abstinence from existence; this means that in any catastrophe I have nothing to lose, and can only gain a consummation devoutly to be wished, as you would say; yet not, as you may think, in order to bring my life to an end, but in order to shape it in such a way as may prove conclusive. Do you believe that death is already written into our universe? Do you believe then that there may be a world beyond, beyond the world of the script? I do not believe so. Would even you, Prince Hamlet, be nothing more than a frightened boy in that place? I know of your courage, but there are certain fears that require a special courage, even heroism. Write to me, and be patient.

The Princess of Clèves

Most Noble Lady! Dear Princess!

So, the cunning and incorrigible Marcellus was right! How delightfully disturbed I was, just this moment, to receive your message. This conversation is possible then, and is really taking place — I am actually speaking to the Princess of Clèves; from uncouth, beer-sodden Denmark I can whisper a message to a city unknown to me, a city of blonde and silent women, so that the fustian of a garrulous soldier is permitted to converse with the delicate and sober silks of Colombelles. I send you a message in which my gratitude vies with the most deplorable humiliation, respect with veneration, and meanwhile innocence and connivance conspire together. Our conversation is a provocation, and without question a transgression — or indeed a fault that runs through the universe, and a symptom of its end. Your noble melancholy enhances but does not conceal the decadence of the stage on which you stand. No less than with Denmark, Colombelles exists in an aura that is neither holiness, nor heavenly light or its reflection, but in fact nothing other than the dust of its continuing decline. You write to me about the delightful little note the Count of Nemours sent you and its three spelling mistakes. I envy this boy with his delicate hands, who has been able to sustain himself by means of your "no", who has even proved worthy of the sanction of your refusal, and whose bold hope even had the opportunity of being blessed in the desperation that you desired. I envy him his sleepless nights, his tears, but neither of these so much as your unjustified rejection. And nothing so much as those three spelling mistakes that reveal, behind the swordsman, the frail soul of a mere boy, whose illiterate fingers, lacking the crutches of fine expression, stagger along the high road of the folio only to stumble in the end, and fall into your forgiving arms. Your husband then anticipated his own death; I can confide in you how Ophelia's voice, which was once so shrill, is now also out of tune, how Guildenstern mistakes himself for Rosencrantz[8] — they have such limited personalities — and how vague, if not reticent Horatio is concerning his origins, his studies and even his parents; they are even saying that Polonius[9] may be an unfrocked priest. All this, however, is much less alarming than what is happening to the ghost of my lord and father. We give it that name though I doubt whether this vapour in uniform is truly my parent; and not without good reason. You see, he is nothing but a phantasm, a poor wretch, a non-thing, a breath thickening in the nostrils of draught horses in winter. But how insolent he is, how devious and cunning. Two days ago, shortly after my death, I went looking for him on the castle ramparts and descried his venerable luminescence propped against the battlements; he was leaning out as if to examine the shadows. Slowly, discreetly as one but recently dead, I approached. He did not seem to hear me. Long, long, the moment of discovery! It was no fantasy, it was my father. He walked about, switching himself on and off again, which I have heard certain fish from the ocean's depths know how to effect, in a rhythm that appeared quite irregular. I paused, in my surprise, and was then disturbed. There could be no doubt; the cunning old ancient was modulating his ill-starred light to serve as a signal. I sharpened my gaze but in the great diurnal night I could see no further than the battlements. Slowly, I withdrew. The old man came down to dinner at the usual hour, but seemed somehow thinner, grief-stricken and worn down; his eyes, however, betrayed signs of wickedness and guile, perhaps even amusement, and he managed a few witticisms with my mother, with whom his relationship is usually very strained. It was precisely this signalling by my father that precipitated my decision to write to you, since I suspect that the old mole,[10] this devious master of intrigue, had in mind some audacious stratagem of which I was entirely ignorant, but which could not be anything of good import if it brought a twisted smile to those thin lips. He has an inclination towards buffoonery, and derision too, nor does he ever refrain from over-acting his part. I feel sure I have noticed, during our formal discussions, a touch of annoyance in him, a troubled impatience when he treats me as a son, as if this were a sort of jape, a sport to be brought quickly to an end. So, my argument runs thus: if my father is signalling, he is conversing with someone; that person would be either alive, or a ghost — one of us, assuming I am alive, or one from the other worlds if a ghost. But are there then other worlds which can provide my penetrable ancestor with persons with whom he may converse? Or is something happening during the night of which we have not the slightest intimation? Is the moaning that can be heard from the spaces far above us or far below the atmosphere of death or of a new life which is foreign to us and incompatible with our lives? Are new monsters preparing to take our place? Might the phantom not then be a more efficient and practical indication of a new life impiously giving birth to itself, rather than being the remains of a life that has already been used up? I think of myself as a real phantom, a unicorn, in comparison with this dishonest deceased being, this grease-paint soul, rapier-proof and eternal, who is already winking at one of his own kind. Could these phantoms be coming to us from the future?

Reply, I entreat you.

Noble Prince,

Your disquiet disquiets me. Your ghosts fill me with wonder and with awe. You should know that here we have no phantoms, but I doubt whether their absence simplifies our situation; perhaps it complicates it. Here we have deaths that are conclusive, not to mention acts of piety, tales of miracles and fables about the gods. So too acts of contrition and veneration, dedication and silence, prayers and ceremonies, all of which are majestic and full of grace. But there is no monster to give all this any meaning or supply a boundary to the summary map of our world. How mean, dreary, fragile and silent it is. While our syntax may be less imaginative than yours, we shape it more thoughtfully. Furthermore, my husband also delivers a most beautiful disquisition on his deathbed, the Duke of Nemours luxuriates in courtly eloquence and the headstrong Duke of Guise overdoes his adjectives; he is green and not likely to mature. Everything you write to me about carries the mournful stench of truth; death no longer knows how to preserve us, stuffed full as it is with foreign matter. And we do not know where that comes from. Yes, we ourselves are in the process of dying, and are already sloughing off our outward forms; these wings encumber us as we ascend or descend, or perhaps both simultaneously, towards some inaccessible region, not knowing whether we travel through majestic heights or precipitous depths. Should we hoist once more our faded heraldry, dear prince? Have you realised that we two, with our antique graciousness, are drawing near to our end, I, busy with my stale works of piety and unflinching in my gaze before the Duke of Nemours's tormented immaturity, you with your honest sword of rhetoric and your lawyers' and theologians' arguments? Strange happenings visit us too: the natural emblems of decadence conjoin with the signs of unease which seems to have no effect on our remorseful servants or our tiresome family members — but during the very same night our messages cross each other in passing. Does it not make monsters of us that the night has opened up to assist our voices? And is it not the case that what you call our provocation has been foreseen in the plans of those beings that are invading our space, or by that unique being who is stealing into it — "being", or should we say "non-being"?

Even the priests are showing signs of concern. They are afraid. But they should understand that their destruction will be every bit as pious as their victory, for is that not so? Why resist? Why not descend into our nothingness protected by the rich caparison of "no", for that indeed is indestructible. Oh, Prince Hamlet, you have no patience, or else you would have been able to understand what was meant when I said "no" to the Duke of Nemours, wouldn't you? You at least, noble prince.

Most Noble Princess,
I know now why the enchantments of my fancy, which I regard as philosophical and, in their way, metaphysical, induced me to write to you more than anyone else. The reason is because you are wholly on the side of death. I would even venture to call you death incarnate; and most assuredly death should have blonde hair like yours, and your fair complexion. I love — allow me this word that burns to caress a form made more out of nothing than of ice — I love the patience with which you have worked to shape your face into an imperishable mask of death, just as you have made your marriage bed into a sarcophagus, and a necropolis of Colombelles. For you, death is a quiet thing; in Denmark the means we employ are more clumsy

and far noisier. There is not one of us here who knows how to change their face into a patient emblem of wax which preserves like a trapped insect the shadow of a smile: its self-denying flesh is half keepsake, half souvenir. What is most charming about your approach to dying is the studied mood of artificiality with which you go about it. That the end of the world should have a fragrance so refined, so expertly innocent!

No, the ghost of my father is not on the side of death. Quite the contrary. As you have clearly understood, he is one of the others, even if I am denied any knowledge of who these "others" might be. Last night I lay in wait by a little tower, from where I could see anyone who should come out to the battlements. Now, it was before midnight when my father appeared on the narrow walkway. I saw him halt, lean forward, and then slowly change the intensity of his luminescence; in the distance I made out a not dissimilar light, but I would say one that was more restless and king-like; to its sudden and fitful variations — which altered from sallow to rose, and from violet to a marvellously luminous black — the ghost responded with dim, slow glimmerings, moving from false pearl to a fugitive, violent yellow, shades of colour which harboured something of supplication or disapproval. On occasion it seemed to me that I saw flashes of deeper colours imbued with anger and an impotent quick temper. There was never any doubt that this was a conversation, and it was enough to persuade me that this transparent being had falsely assumed the character of my father,[11] and that it was a profligate, a creature of the underworld, a spy or perhaps the killer of some goat-like god hidden in the crevices of space.

But in your world there are no phantoms, only letters of love. As for us, our exceptional love letters are brim-full of arrogance and the bitterness of grief. We invent a god for ourselves, and not without good reason, judging from the iniquitous acts that abound here below. And we imagine that there are universes without a god, or others in which there are many or in which there are one or many devils in charge of things. There can be no doubt that this sense of foreboding, this calm confusion, had its origins in the chamber where the gods make their penitence. I am determined to disobey my god, and in so doing you suppose I am obeying some god who is further beyond, so that my defiance is in fact still obedience. But in this way I come to learn the bitter joy of disobedience, and teach the god beyond that I cannot be relied upon. You may object that, in this instance, disobedience corresponds to death, and by that you certainly do not mean the emblematic death about which we soliloquise every day, but absolute death. I wonder whether there could not be a way of escaping this death in order to conspire in further acts of unpardonable disobedience.

Noble Prince,

Your mind is clearly troubled by reckless hopes and immoderate excitements which are a source of danger just as much as anxiety. Certainly, there is no danger so great that it would dissuade a person from talking about his own or another's death. But I fear that your agitation may prompt you to some caprice or folly that would not so much make our deaths as nothing, or render them void in advance, as damage them in some other way. The fact that you boast of disobeying your god is already reckless, and also impious, although that in itself does not speak of a want of nobility. Yet why fantasise about an act of defiance which would be so radical as to challenge the very permanence of the gods beyond? And what is more, even if you were able to find a way or a stratagem for blaspheming these other gods, it would resolve nothing at all. Would not these gods, in fact, merely enclose themselves within other gods even further beyond, as if the whole universe were constructed as a series of divine containers, in such a way that the destruction of some gods might allow others to come forward who are increasingly larger, so to speak, each of whom might contain a succession of other gods that tend towards the infinitely small? Perhaps too, even we, we gods of nothing but gods in some way nevertheless, will give way in turn to forms of nothing that are somehow more elaborately fashioned, more complete or more comprehensive? Why then disobey? Isn't a disobedience conducted within obedience more ingenious? Is there not power in silent restraint, in maintaining a resolute quiescence before death? You must realise that my "no" to the Duke of Nemours was also intended to be a definitive "no" to the gods beyond and not a simple expression of disobedience. I think it was a noble scheme of mine, to employ an incomprehensible "no" to bestow nobility upon a worldly situation, while at the same time alluding, and not without a certain dignified anger, to another case, also worldly but in a different way — I will not say otherworldly. Your passion fascinates me, but, as you say, I am resolutely on the side of death.

Most Noble Princess,
This universe may indeed be constructed as you suppose, with gods that contain other gods, and I further surmise that this conversation of ours may be proof that now, at least one such flaw, a bloodless wound and fissure, has become wide enough to allow commerce between one universe and another; it may also be that the administrators of the world to come are developing a plan for a compulsory federation of cosmoses. In order for us to communicate we must inveigle ourselves into this small bubble of time, like two souls seeking a bubble of life that is contemporaneous so as to practise their requited love. Our conversation touches on the imminent end of the world, which, as you point out, is also its beginning. So be it. Yet I feel no love nor interest for those other gods beyond who will take the place of the gods of today. I loathe these parasitic overseers and have only contempt for those who give succour to these moribund bit-players with their

phosphorescent entrails. The gods may be magnificent and powerful, but they are so stupid! I want to hunt them down, to shame them, insult them and deceive them; above all, to *defy* them.

    Noble Prince,

The gods are merely powerful, but in order for them to acquire dignity they must grow old, since dignity is the privilege of those who are conscious of their mortality. We, now and only now, are so much better than the gods. Let us teach them dignity, through that unique lexicon which is all that remains to us — our death.

    Noble Princess,

Each day I find such consolation in your letters! I cannot agree with a single word you say, but that is presumably a familiar situation for you, is it not? I reject every word you write, but would run my rapier through anyone who dared call you a liar. I contradict you, and so we come to confront each other, with our faces at the same level. You fascinate me. Your "no" is more deadly than any "yes". I don't want a "yes" from you; all I want is what you are willing to give me, whatever that may be. But let it come from you. At the present moment, we are not alone in knowing this — that the end of the world is very near. Today a fissure opened in the water in which Ophelia drowns every day. No one mentioned it. Ophelia's funerals have become a scene of frenetic buffoonery, while the duel is now a wild affair of swordplay and butchery.[12] The only one who knows anything about what is going on is that degenerate ghost, but it would be pointless, perhaps even disastrous, to question him. I am keeping an eye out — I have witnessed another of those nocturnal "colloquies". As I write a fierce wind rakes the towers, and Denmark no more finds relief, not even in *aqua vitae*.

Noble Prince,

So we are keeping a diary then, of the days before the end of the world? I shall, with youthful diligence, note down my earthquakes as if they were lines from some *billets doux*, wherein the lightning bolts were like unto glances and the torn sky's wounds the heartbeats of my beloved, and the flight of slow, ill-omened birds are a foreshadowing of letters of love. I will take catastrophe and make it into the diary of a young virgin girl. The Devil will find me seated at the spinet, or rapt in tying ribbons around old letters. I am happy and content today, a quite unusual thing for me. In your letters there is a confusion that would displease any purist, but not a woman of good sense. I listen to what you say with interest and reverence, but also disapproval and amusement. Thanks to you, the ashes of Judgement Day will take on many hues. Regards.

Noble Princess,

Confusion, confusion! Our prattling has stirred up the monsters of the abyss. Marcellus, the fool, has talked. The reckless queen wishes to lay her hands on the verbal catapult, the king too desires to play around with it. Tonight, the troubled remains of my father came to find me. He was looking at the apparatus with a greedy expression, and perhaps also despair. Invoking his paternal authority, the old rogue — though but a thing of air — stretched out his hands as if appealing to be able to make use of it, but I held him at bay with all manner of offensive exorcisms. To his angry supplications I responded, "Who were you conversing with the other night...?" Just those words. I saw him grow pale, as far as that is possible for a ghost, until he became quite transparent, though withered and dark, and trembled, the depraved nothing that he was, and rolled his eyeless gaze. I will hide the apparatus where it cannot be found. I shall resume this letter later on.

Three o'clock — everyone is asleep, only the phantom is about, but it seems unlikely he would dare venture this far. The queen, that miserable woman, would like to communicate, most likely to some killer or brigand, a man who would disappoint the wishes of a deceitful mother.[13] She will not touch this contraption; or I would run her through with something sharper than words. Yet this unfortunate discovery has turned their hearts bitter. Poor Ophelia looks at me with such an expression! She supposes that I am conversing with distant beings, as in fact is the case, but in her old-fashioned naivety she fantasises that those distant beings might thus be nearer to the other gods, precisely because they are so far away. But she does not know that it is forbidden for the gods to be close to anything except that place from which all distances themselves originate.

Most Noble Lady,

I write to you in furious haste, after a heated conversation with my father who was being careful, so he declared, to speak openly and seriously. No sooner had I finished my previous message than a radiance at my side gave me to understand that I was among family. There beside me was the household comet, my consanguineous candle and rocket of my ancestor, looking gaunt, haggard and shaking somewhat — there was a hint of terror in one eye, and in the other the remnants of proud reproach. His speech was decked out with metaphors, exhortations and dramatic pauses, together with noble perorations and ingenious appeals to the emotions; all this was delivered in a voice as plaintive as the wind, sometimes proudly but not so much that it concealed a hidden pain that was perhaps not simulated. And anyone who succeeded in clearing a way through these rough thickets of eloquence would have discovered a tale not dissimilar to the one I now relate:

"I have played the spectre of your father for such a long time now that I have gradually become convinced that I *am* this particular character. I only realised recently how far I had taken this tragic deception, although I do not wish to blame myself more than is just, since as far as we unnaturals are concerned lying is as normal for us as dreaming is for you, or loving, killing and all the other immaterial aberrations of materiality. I belong to that race of spirits of mines, bogs, caves and caverns who derive their sustenance from the fungi and subtle lichens to be found in the shadows, or from the ashes and fossils of imaginary animals and imitation vegetables. There is no vein or fissure in the Earth," the old crook went on, not without a touch of professional pride, "that does not crawl with us, with wordless and lustrous swarms of us. Our situation is rather odd since it casts us in a tragic role, which is all the more grandiose as it is clearly quite useless. The specific nature of our condition derives from the fact that we simply do not acknowledge death. All our mishaps, all our troubles, all our pitiful and pitiable perversions which make us everywhere repugnant and altogether wretched, all of these proceed from this condition of immortality.

"Not one of us is the ghost of a dead man — in fact the dead don't have ghosts. So you will appreciate that we must devote all our energy to a complex process of synthesis in order to present ourselves as participants in the process of death. Lacking any definite form, and without that coat of arms which alone can establish our heraldic compliance, being denied colours, symbols or pennants, we knights, who whilst not cowardly have grown indolent during our cosmic misadventure that has endured for centuries, for ever, have devised — or did someone else propose it? — this ruse, this stratagem, one that is not ignoble at that but in fact rather clever in a macabre sort of way. So, since we are denied the advantages of an active death, and do not dare to aspire to the geometric delights of being clad in heraldic colours, we attempt, through an adultery that is both unholy and sacred, to enjoy someone else's demise, to wrest passion from a deathbed, and take possession of a false identity. In this way we loathsome — though not pitiless — vampires who prey upon the already-dead fraudulently put on their clothes, memorise their past loves, their fears and the agonies of their despair; we take note of the treacheries that led to our victims' deaths and then misappropriate their revenge; by means of rhetorical "appearances" we keep alive their memory, and make it menacing for those who are soon to be dead, whose dregs of conscience we stir up; we oppress people's dreams and sleep, already disturbed as they are by guilt and lechery, cause curtains to move and fill your empty halls with cries of agony that resound with accusation — and with good reason. Conversions, acts of faith, sudden transfigurations: behind these events, the regular fodder of the gutter press, our sure touch will always be recognisable. Likewise astrological predictions, minor miracles, warnings, tricks played by gypsies who travel between the spheres or tireless swindlers. Everything I said about your uncle, and about your mother, is all perfectly true, as if that matters to you," the poor ghost continued, like a drunk but honest accountant who perceives that his disreputable professional honesty is under suspicion, "although I should add that the deception inclined somewhat towards my own interest in this rather distressing tale.[14] Dearest Hamlet, it was me who urged you to take revenge, a revenge that was of no specific interest to me, but which set in motion an unstoppable machine and created a form into which I could infuse myself, thereby supplying a means for me to acquire a destiny, albeit one that was second class. For us, the only way of procuring a mortal state is to suck the destiny out of someone else. So I was lying, like a smooth-tongued commercial traveller, when I went into such detail about my sufferings in the abyss; or rather, I translated them into something other than what they really were, because you cannot imagine, young man," and here he stared at me with the desperate bitterness of a vicious old lecher, "what it means to be shorn of death, and destiny."

He took a deep breath, folded the glowing stumps of his arms, then started to speak again, but this time in quite a different tone: less tormented, but, I would say, more menacing, as if he were gripped by a baleful resolve.

"You will be aware, by now, and it will not come as a revelation that takes your breath away to learn that things have reached a state of crisis. This universe of yours is falling apart, your escutcheons are being overwhelmed by those of others while swords are being replaced by new devices which are insidiously disastrous and lacking in any quality of heroism. The gods are dying under the weight of their chronic obesity, angels hover awkwardly over fortune's wheel, shedding feathers from their wings, and the very water is breaking up and swirling away, so that it is no longer deep enough for Ophelia to drown her face in it. Our fates are diverging: it falls to you, to all those who have a destiny, to destroy your heraldic tinctures completely — your red, green and black, your lions rampant, your king of diamonds, bishops and rooks. For us it is different, the chessboard upon which we find ourselves is slipping away from beneath us; the castle flags hang limp and the crows are losing their appetite. I must leave you, and begin the quest for another destiny upon which to feast. And that is no easy matter; for until some foothold can be found, a stalactite or a concealed finger of rock where we can perch, we will fly around aimlessly like winged moles on the edge of existence. Does it surprise you that even amidst all these forewarnings of catastrophe I should be trying to smuggle myself into yet one more performance? You caught me by surprise that time when I was speaking, in my usual manner, with one who has some authority in our world and who has, we suspect, some knowledge, perhaps only a glimpse, of a world to come. This person is working assiduously to compile a census of all us subterraneans and is trying to arrange a cosmic transfer for us, but it seems that organising those like me or who share my background presents a number of difficulties. Apparently we are a bit too specialised, and, on the other hand, it seems the game of impersonating the recent dead is almost at its end. See what I mean? I should move on, maybe learn another trade, something a little more respectable and less demanding. The night Horatio doesn't recognise my form out on the terrace you will know that the end has come. I have seen your toy," he continued, in a circumspect yet knowing voice, "what messages one might send with a gadget such as that! But where do they go? There must be cracks in the universe through which they escape," he concluded, his voice now hoarse, "if only we could find them!"

He withdrew, leaving me in a state of utter bewilderment.

Noble Prince,

I was extremely moved when I read the tale of your poor ghost, and it is a very long time since I read anything so touching and so full of pathos.

It seems our premonition that the very fabric of the universe is on the point of breaking up was not without foundation. I am inclined to believe it, with as much composure as I am able to muster. In the faint but still perceptible ease of our conversation some intimate hesitation has intruded, an ambiguous and subtle allusion — perhaps some day I will speak to you of it.

Noble Princess!

Do not betray me, I beseech you — it is I, Ophelia. I have been able to lay hands on Marcellus's mechanism and am sending you a message, in haste, so that Hamlet does not discover me. No, I shall not betray your secret, nor tell anybody where the prince conceals this device, oh princess! For some time — I suppose since he took up writing to you — Hamlet has been in a fearfully disturbed condition; his behaviour is at once overbearing and pathetic, and while I have known him a long time I have never seen him so quick to sneer or prone to tears. I think I understand: his heart has changed. He no longer loves me and is aware that this makes his portrayal of Hamlet inauthentic. He responds to my death with indifference, makes a feeble job of killing Laertes, yet maintains, complicitly and even perversely, a notable degree of respect for the ghost of his lord and father. It does not upset me that he has become estranged from me, but it *does* worry me that all this should be happening now, when the horses of the Apocalypse — our own little apocalypse, but for all that a perfectly respectable apocalypse — are battering their hooves on the pavement of the sky, that our eternal work has become corrupted and our escutcheon sullied, and that I am entering into my nothingness alone, this nothingness that allows affinities and yet imposes loneliness; it worries me too that he makes his entrance unaccompanied, lying to himself out loud, at once brave but cowardly, shouting, groaning and threatening, like a boy who is afraid and raging against the dark. We had constructed for ourselves a nuptial sarcophagus, and if no single wedding-sheet awaited us then at least we would have had a single shroud; a first night together that would last for ever — not the oblivion longed for by those who are newly wed but sufficient to overwhelm any living creature, an embracing of our non-existence that would compose together at last an escutcheon in negative, the ultimate in blazonry, formed of the heraldic tinctures of the void. Now, however, all this is threatened, perhaps already irretrievably compromised. Princess! Perhaps one word from you would be enough to give us, in these final headlong hours, the consolation of a Hamlet as strange and melancholy as ever, but a Hamlet who is ours! Will you please send me a reply?

    Dear Ophelia

I have no knowledge of how a well-raised young woman of your rank would be addressed in Denmark, and so I hope you will allow me to speak to you in this manner. Although our experience is different, we are sisters in our shared denial. Hamlet's letters have demonstrated to me that the prince is disturbed, yet for some reason he will not admit such a conclusion, not out of any vain desire for survival, but owing to his desire to attribute some element of defiance to his character. He wishes to say "no", but the difference between him and us is that, unlike we women who understand the eternal reciprocity between birth and death, he supposes that disobeying amounts to the simple act of saying "no". He is a man of courage but lacks judgement, and the grief he is causing you in these decisive times indicates the depth of his confusion. Oh how I too would love a double sarcophagus constructed of shadows! But do you think that "nothingness" suits a fair complexion? I will speak to your poor Hamlet.

Princess,

I am replying immediately and shall keep to the point. I did not dare say to you what was in my mind, nor take the step from which there would be no return — which would even cause the sarcophagus to shatter; I did not tell you what I suspect and what I fear — that Hamlet loves you and realises that he loves you. Oh God!

Noble Princess,

Please do not be concerned. I have surprised dear Ophelia in the act of sending you a message, and caught sight of the last line. I feel no anger towards my Ophelia, my companion in this dusk of cold fire. What she told you — the poor girl is weeping in despair at my side, but I will not reproach her — is true. I love you and I know that I love you. What use is there in lying? Every letter could be our last — every word even. The distance that separates us cannot be crossed; the night is absolute and there are no stars for us to see; should we not give thanks to chance or destiny for these dialogues of love? Of my own feelings I know somewhat more: they are not linked to this world, and are not of the flesh, nor in essence sentimental. They are allegorical. The war which in some way is being fought — we know not where, though we see the signs of it and suspect we see its conclusion — is a war of allegories. My love for you is a device from the past, a chorus of personifications and a struggle between images exquisitely inscribed on scrolls; it resembles Dialectics, Mathematics and Astronomy — and these I employ to fill the space that separates Hamlet from the Princess of Clèves. In the chaos of the Apocalypse the Unicorn's charge stands vacant. The Earthly Paradise burns, but its outlines can still be discerned; and it is cold. In the sky that has been designed for us, there is a place for a Woman in the abstract, one who is blonde, silent and dead.

Noble Prince,

I read your letter with some emotion, and will not hide from you that which only the coming end and the insurmountable distance between us can unseal from my lips; although I do not love you, I feel deeply involved in the allegory of which you speak; if Unicorns exist then that must mean that there is also a Lady of the Unicorn, and she too, as you well know, was accustomed to making denials. Our allegory then is a "no" as intricately illuminated as an initial, so skilfully woven and resplendent that it is as secret and imposing as the manuscript of our sky, for only an expert eye could detect its outline. Yet I would like to suggest to you, my distant friend, a more far-reaching allegory; Ophelia is in need of an allegory too, so you should conceive of one that is large enough to accommodate the two of you, and perhaps, the two of us. Do not relinquish that nuptial sarcophagus. This "no" demands a nymph, a creature of the water, one who is at ease with suffering and madness. There are many degrees of death and Ophelia is in greater danger than we are.

Princess,

Hamlet has permitted me to speak with you again. I heard your last message and while I see that your project is well meaning, I also understand that what awaits us is our own funeral niche of shadows, each one quite distinct, and separated by an impassable distance from each other. No one can rely on a sarcophagus being so well made that its white night of marble will protect against that other invincible night. I accept my suffering; I too am a nymph of denial. The allegory in which we may include ourselves allows for us to retain our forms, but only with all three of us facing outwards; thus our forms will not be aware of each other, nor will they ever know how close to one another they are. I shall not write to you again. I thank you and kiss your hands.

Noble Princess,

In these last hours, when our great scheme unravels in an increasingly disjointed and catastrophic manner, there is something in Ophelia's attitude, her particular subtlety, that baffles me. I assent to loving you within the bounds of the allegory because in this way I receive from you a kind of allegorical acceptance. But I lack patience. Today I struck the queen my mother and felt glad to have done so. For years I have longed to slap her face, as hard as I could. She wanted the verbal catapult, this stupid woman and avid reader of Bromfield and Cronin.[15] I had another conversation with my father, who was elusive and showed no trace of emotion; I wonder if he has secured some accommodation. The ineluctable is very close.

Dear Ophelia,

I can find no words to tell you how much your letter troubles me. Virgin widow! I envy you the youthfulness of your "no".

Noble Prince,

How strange these conversations are that speed through space, at such a time! My peace of mind, if it has not been destroyed, has certainly become disturbed; I am suffering from a restless drowsiness and would not wish it on you at all. Yesterday I had a long discussion with my dead husband, during which he found a way of telling me something about himself, something that has a little bearing on our situation, and will interest you I feel sure.

"I suppose that, even though you have never asked me, you have sometimes asked yourself why — knowing that I have been neither loved nor desired by you, but that you are free from that spite, anger and impatience which are somehow capable of combining into a kind of affection — why in the end I wished to marry you. To this question, and your silence does not contradict what I have supposed, I would like to respond. In short, I married you precisely because you did not love or desire me; because you were in a state of utter composure, reluctance and denial." That last was the actual word he used, which intrigued me beyond measure. "This state of 'no' was so fundamental, even if unspoken, that it led me to hope that at your side I might experience that condition of stable yet turbulent equilibrium which I know may otherwise only be experienced in death. Of necessity I had to behave as a husband, but only so that would not involve you in this choice of mine, which had to remain unspoken in order to prevent the sacred absurdity and deep-seated fraud of it from coming to light. I had always wanted to live a life without love or sensuality, one that was wholly abstract, or better yet, killed off; at the same time, however, I understood that this magnificent work of absence, this fiction or representation of death, could be celebrated only by surrendering the entire structure of my life to prevarication. It's easy, and simple enough to die, but so much more impetuous to develop a life that has the density and coherence of death; it is easy not to love, though dangerous to attach the absence of love to a creature supremely worthy of that love, or to use a desirable body to sustain abstinence, and turn elsewhere for pleasure. Alas, you were but a simulation of death; you were capable of loving and desire. This it was that killed me. I was supposed to have died out of jealousy; for the sake of consistency I chose instead to die from a despair based on suspicions which I openly disguised as no more than worldly. In fact, I was able to tolerate the man you loved much more easily than your proclivity for love itself. Had you fallen in love with me, I would have died out of sheer disgust. When I discovered you were unfaithful in your devotion to absence, I wanted to die. My action was cowardly, without a doubt, and resembled the act of writing out a word-for-word translation of an untranslatable text: for 'the representation of death' I substituted 'a death of representation'."

This "confession"[16] of my poor husband's did not surprise me, and I replied to him in approximately these terms: that I had understood exactly his reasons for choosing me as his wife; and that, although my destiny could not wholly contribute towards his own, nevertheless I had tried to cooperate, giving it my complete and considered attention. I explained to him how I had used the fact that I had fallen in love as a way of putting myself in the position of denial. Since he had married me in order to enjoy the chastity of death, I had adopted a strategy in relation to my own passion that was equally negative. For my "no" to be truly on the side of death, I had to assume the mannerisms and the bloom of life. A whiteness tinted with blood. A tenderness that could carve the marble of a sepulchre. A kiss that represented adultery as a wedding, and married life as a funeral.

"Your death," I added finally, "gave me a way of carrying this mortal virtue of mine to its conclusion. On your deathbed I clearly saw the intermediate moves that would allow me to utter, at the end, my perfect, my supreme 'no'."

"So," my husband replied, "my death was but a move that contributed to your ultimate victory."

"No," I replied, "my life and your death were both moves made in the service of 'no'."

Most Noble Princess,

How profound were my feelings upon reading your letter, although, I grant you, they were merely the expression of my passions and impatience. Yet when I write that I love you, please appreciate that I am talking about a love granted only by catastrophe, by this dawn which masquerades as dusk. Princess, I will never be able to unwind you out of your shroud of shadow. Ophelia sends you her regards; I am fascinated by the deep and forthright way in which her thoughts proceed. The allegory is at work — *your* allegory! With what affection, how graciously, the ice-cold "no" wraps us in its impossible arms.

Noble Prince,

With the agreement of the princess, in fact with her active encouragement, I am entrusting a short and heart-felt message to the verbal catapult. I am the Duke of Nemours. My task is not to understand, and I have gone about this duty, which was not easy, nor always honourable, with patience and integrity. I do not understand much of what you have been saying about "no" — at least not in the way I am used to understanding — but I do know that I have always devoted myself to the princess, and if the princess deigned — please forgive the expression — to choose me, this meant that I was a suitable collaborator in her project, being the only one capable of receiving and accepting her refusal with the dull desolation and reliable, steadfast cooperation her nature required. Without me, without my impoverished destiny and my propensity to mislay it as easily as someone losing a glove at a ball, her "no" would never have resulted in this obscure insight which I can fathom only in its rudiments. Now something is casting doubt upon our symbolic survival itself. Prince: if we belonged to the same world, by this stage I would have challenged you without mercy unto death; not out of hatred or jealousy, but solely because your life seems incompatible with the tenor of my own. No need to mention Ophelia; my destiny is more impoverished than hers; indeed, it would be more accurate to say that I scarcely have a destiny, since I am clinging to this precarious narrative quite desperately, and already drifting into "nothingness". You are propelling me towards this "nothingness". I now look upon the whole of my existence with despair.

Prince,

Were I to pretend that ours is a single universe, as you desire I should, then I would agree to my body being pierced through by you, for in no circumstances would I ever direct my rapier against a person upon whom our dear princess looks so favourably. Our universes, which are fundamentally incompatible, have come into contact with each other only because something, either out there in the beyond or within, has been shattered, and so our two worlds, such as they were, no more exist. Yet had our worlds endured as they did formerly, we would never have met one another, and mutual jealousy would not have been our fate. Your destiny is destroyed, and is itself breaking apart the very structure of the world. It was not I who destroyed it. But in this repect your terror is unfounded, because for some time already you have been hurtling through space. Be of good spirit. Soon everything will be clear — or else wrapped in darkness entirely.

Noble Princess,

My father has gone! We have turned our ramshackle castle upside-down, and must now accept that death is imminent. We pretended to remain calm when discussing who could be trusted to act as his stand-in. Most of us were for Rosencrantz, that wan fellow with the face of a corpse, but I immediately saw what a mistake that would be. We might as well have all thrown ourselves into the grave. I argued that my father's absence should not be filled, but this still left a role to be played, and I suggested the king perform it. For a moment there was some bewilderment. The king blanched, then accepted, in a faint voice. The accuracy of my suggestion struck everyone immediately. If the king is both the ghostly accuser and the victim who appeases him,[17] then everything makes sense again. We have thus discovered an unforeseen escutcheon, and have raised it up above the gates of our ruined castle.

Noble Prince,

I am writing to you in a state of some anxiety, to inform you of an event that will not fail to disturb you. Your father has arrived here among us. My husband having died just a few hours earlier, a faint glimmer pervaded the room now shaken by my weeping. At first I chose to ignore this strange gleam, convinced that it was merely another sign of the approaching catastrophe. But the glow persisted, and took on the form of an ancient warrior in arms who, with uncouth enunciation and stumbling, as if spelling out the words, addressed me: "You want a ghost?" In response to the pallor which had doubtless spread across my face the figure added, with an astonishing lack of refinement, "There's a corpse here. If you want a ghost, I'm your man." I muttered something, feeling totally disconcerted and at a loss to understand. And this fellow, equally amazed and annoyed, continued, "Aren't you the Princess of Clèves?" I replied in the affirmative to which he replied, "I'm Hamlet's father. You've heard a lot about me." Taking no notice of my obvious state of mind, he added, "I've got out of that other place. I know you've got your own troubles too, but I only need a few hours. Any job you like. Be off again in a day or so." I implored him not to make himself visible. I promised that I would think of something for him. He seemed suspicious at this, it seemed to me. The situation is exceedingly embarrassing. I shudder at the thought that someone might discover him.

Princess,

I am distraught and dismayed. Your courtesy, and our correspondence, have together proved disastrous. Evidently the old scoundrel must have picked up some idle talk about you, and had clearly been keeping an eye on me. But how on earth was he able to locate your universe? Did he have access to Marcellus's calculations?

Prince,

Now that my dismay has ebbed a little, I must say that your father's arrival has failed to bring about the upset I had expected. If I am honest, your father, with that air of his that recalls a dubious mariner ever on the look-out for illicit gains and profitable schemes, has a certain quality about him that pleases me. At this hour, when time races on in precipitate acceleration, even the Princess of Clèves can allow herself, like a country girl, to converse with this clumsy, ill-mannered man, this "non-man" who is so well versed in human intrigue and subterfuge. I chatted with him for quite some while; he spoke of you with a rough, rather than warm admiration. Eventually I asked him how he had managed to find, then reach, our universe. He looked at me as if the question was really too extreme an example of female simple-mindedness. "With the word-catapult, how else! Do you think I weigh much more than a sentence?" In my view this comment showed little sympathy for your style of prose.

Noble Princess,
Oh, miserable, wretched, fantastical and conceited fool that I am! The word-catapult — it was so obvious! But Hamlet is not always so careless, it must be said. Princess, I am writing to you in the throes of desperate emotion; I am sweating, quivering like a horse at the end of a race, a race of utter panic — and hope. Princess, I have decided, with the help of my feeble mathematics, to attempt the construction of a verbal catapult capable of conveying — me! Princess, it will be up to us, and not our gods, to bring about the ruin of the world.

Prince!
Your proposal disturbs me. In your excitement I perceive a wildness, a murderous and suicidal ecstasy, that fills me with amazement and perhaps also terror. It is not for us, with our own hands, to bring about the end of our universes. They are already dying; even their deaths are on the point of dying in one single death. The action that you intend to carry out is not so much courageous as terrifying, deadly and altogether impossible to undo. Rash fantasy! This is disobedience beyond any forgiveness. I implore you: accept the common lot, without anger, gladly even. Do not attempt to destroy the heavens.

Princess,

How charmingly you seek to dissuade me! But can there be anything more persuasive than so indulgent a dissuasion? When you say that this is a momentous disobedience, you certainly have a point. Is this then the new "no" that will take the place of the old "no", the final confrontation with the gods of the end of it all? Is it possible we might work together on this "no"? I am at work already, and feverishly preparing myself. In only a few hours the king has become a most excellent ghost, but the torment of his double role and the conflicting feelings of remorse are wearing him down. I should be ready by tomorrow evening.

Prince,

Think, think again on the consequences of your actions. Your arrival in our universe would be an event beyond everyone's comprehension, except mine and your father's. It spells not only death, but death without meaning. Do we have the right to bleed the meaning from this dying world in order to invent a new meaning?

Princess,

A new meaning? What else? What more than that dare I ask for?

Prince,

My heart breaks to send you this message, which may be my last. Our world has come to an end. Your father, falling short of his promised discretion, has already established himself as the ghost of my husband and is now intent on setting up a dictatorship which will be as despicable as it will be unyielding. He has cobbled together a tale that speaks of a rotten Denmark and a piteous Colombelles, a mockery and insult on both our houses. And this he means to impose on us as our destiny. Fear and dismay have left me paralysed along with the rest of those here. In spite of my own feelings I have no option but to beseech you to make your journey. We are about to lose the death to which we are entitled.

Princess,

Have faith! Pile insults on him. Remind him of his lowly origins, the merest smattering of humanity that remains to him. If he is acting in this way he must be on his last legs. To patch together stories such as those! What next, old mole! He must have a destiny, he's raging and delirious. Shuffle the lines, swap roles, undermine his crass scheming and intimidate him. Feign indulgence; it will drive him into ecstasies. And now — I dare speak with you no more.

Princess,

I have discovered on my desk — this is Horatio — a strange letter from Hamlet which informs me of the incredible story of your conversations in the darkest of shadows. He also writes that he has constructed a device by means of which he proposes to come to you. He adds that by the time I am reading this he will already have left. All of this confers on our catastrophe a touch of the ludicrous, the burlesque, I might almost say the music hall. I am not sure why I am sending you this message. If you should chance to see our noble and melancholy prince, tell him that we miss him, but that soon we will feel that loss no more. The night thickens, the things of the daytime are falling into decay… I do not reproach you in the least.

Noble Horatio,

Your letter fills me with extreme anxiety. Hamlet has left... but Hamlet is *not* here. Hamlet has *not* arrived. And as for his father... We are, one and all of us, mired in this ghastly and foetid light.

To the deepest shadows

I am sending this message into the darkness; no one, perhaps, will ever receive it. It will drift on for centuries, beyond all understanding, like a bird whose feathers have been plucked, fluttering about in terror around an aviary with no resting place. Things irreversible are silently taking place in every part of the cosmos. I have left my wooden O, but have failed to reach the realm of velvets. This here is a region of darkness and deep gloom, and all I hear is the ticking of infinite clocks. There is flesh here, but I see no bodies. I have crouched down on the threshold of an unknown sea, featureless and sickly sweet, and am huddled in my costume that now seems so outlandish. I am not dying, I will not die. Oh my princess! Where are they gone, our sarcophagi?

NOTES

1. The "platform" is part of the battlements of the castle of Elsinore, where Hamlet meets his father's ghost, and can also be interpreted as the stage on which the drama is performed (*Hamlet*, I, 2, 213). Manganelli also conceals a number of citations from the play in this text, such as the "wild and whirling" words at the start of this sentence (I, 5, 136).

2. Ophelia and Yorick. Ophelia rejects Hamlet's love, on her father's advice, but in her grief at Hamlet's strange behaviour and following the death of her father she loses her mind and drowns herself. Yorick was the court jester, whose skull is unearthed in the graveyard scene (*Hamlet*, V, 1, 170-191). The next phrase is an echo of Hamlet's "How weary, stale, flat and unprofitable/Seem to me all the uses of this world" (I, 2, 133-134).

3. One of the few examples where Manganelli uses a direct quotation from *Hamlet*, from the "To be, or not to be" soliloquy; the consummation wished for is death (*Hamlet*, III, 1, 64-65).

4. Hamlet encounters the ghost at a later hour: "twixt eleven and twelve/I'll visit you" (*Hamlet*, I, 2, 250-251).

5. The princess retreats to her chateau at Coulommieres, but Manganelli changes its name in his text, presumably to distance it from its source (*The Princesse de Clèves*, trans. Terence Cave, Oxford University Press, 1999, p.92).

6. The princess is demonstrating to Hamlet that she is aware of Shakespeare's drama, by alluding to Ophelia's comment on his strange behaviour: "O, what a noble mind is here o'erthrown" (*Hamlet*, III, 1, 150).

7. See the Introduction for a brief summary of the roles played by these characters.

8. Rosencrantz and Guildenstern are courtiers, and formerly Hamlet's friends, employed by Claudius to spy on the prince.

9. Ophelia's father, and a senior courtier whom Hamlet kills by accident.

10. One of Hamlet's terms to refer to the ghost (*Hamlet*, I, 5, 161).

11. In *Hamlet* the true nature of the ghost is a source of anxiety since it may truly be his

father's ghost, or else is an evil spirit intent on depriving Hamlet of his sanity (*Hamlet*, I, 4, 39-61).

12. At Ophelia's funeral, her brother Laertes leaps into her grave and then when Hamlet appears he leaps out to attack him because he blames Hamlet for causing his sister's insanity (*Hamlet*, V, 1, 235-247). In the final "duel" scene, his mother the queen dies from drinking poison and Hamlet kills Claudius with a poisoned rapier, which also causes Laertes's death. Finally Hamlet himself dies, also poisoned by the sword (V, 2).

13. Hamlet is particularly disturbed by his mother's hasty marriage to Claudius (*Hamlet*, I, 2, 137-159). He later criticises her at length for being, as he sees it, unfaithful to the memory of his father (III, 4, 7-215).

14. The ghost in "An Impossible Love" is clearly "a goblin damn'd" rather than the true ghost of Hamlet's father, "a spirit of health" (*Hamlet*, I, 4, 40).

15. Louis Bromfield (1896–1956) and A.J. Cronin (1896–1981) were once both highly regarded middle-brow writers, and widely read. Hamlet is apparently disparaging the queen's taste in literature.

16. The most famous section in *The Princess of Clèves* is her confession to her husband that she loves another man. This leads eventually to her husband's death, so his confession here subverts the novel in most respects, since he does not love his wife, for example, and does not die out of jealousy.

17. Hamlet's suggestion involves a reversal of roles. In Shakespeare's play the ghost accuses Claudius, the king, of murdering him, so in Manganelli's text the king, who is here playing the ghost, becomes both accuser and victim.

17. One of Hamlet's terms to refer to the ghost (*Hamlet*, I, 5, 161).

DISQUISITION ON THE DIFFICULTY OF
COMMUNICATING WITH THE DEAD

hat follows is not intended to be a personal contribution to this debate, for I count myself among the lowest of creatures, almost to the point of non-existence; and so, being only too aware of my insignificance and my ignorance, I would never venture in any way to seek the attention of my "peers" (I speak ironically). And anyway, when I have been reduced to a mere catalogue of sewage, an inventory of worms or a taxonomy of whiskers, what will be left of this me to talk about? You see therefore how aware I am of my own being, grounded as it is in nothingness, only removed from being an absolute nothing in so far as it knows itself to be: nothing.

Unsuited to any kind of audacity, whether of mind or of limb, I have committed my mole-like obduracy to this miscellany which I dare to hope proves in some respects to be informative even though it smacks of codices and compendia, of the sweatshop and the monastery. The miserly, short-sighted antiquarian fantasises not of worldly glories or truths that might enlighten us, but allows his work to be reduced to the juxtaposition in glass cabinets of one of Caesar's toenails and an out–of-date stamp, or a letter from Amalasuntha beside some literary compilation, as chance or fate, or the simple foolishness of things dictates. Indeed he would be dismayed to recognise a fingerprint on the thirtieth piece of silver, or Apollo's autograph in a labyrinthine doodle depicting a barren leaf in a note for an oracle.

In the following pages a discussion is put forward on the difficulty of communicating with the dead, often incorporating, for the reader's elucidation, certain hand-written records from those who have dedicated to this enterprise both their hard work and their courage; other pages present summaries and paraphrases following the fancies of my laziness and incurable stupidity; and all of this is set out in a prose that combines paucity of vocabulary and perfunctory grammar with my almost execrably impoverished style. I have dared, on occasion, to murmur to my readers — who may be daydreaming or justifiably impatient with the lack of substance — certain scurfy scribblings which give off the odour of oil lamps; I slip in certain cadaverous commentaries; and all of this I have managed by dipping the feeble quill of my invention into the blackest of midnight inks — in such a way do men act when they set down their dreams, imbuing the very pen-nibs of their selves in the ink-well of night.

I.

Everyone agrees most wholeheartedly that communicating with the dead is a task at once hard to envisage, frightening to contemplate, terrifying to attempt, alarming when completed, and in every respect fraught with anxiety. One must also consider: the warnings and ordinances of the pious, and of the nervous; the nature of the party with whom the dialogue is to be conducted — elusive, tight-lipped, distant, or almost completely worn down, practically non-existent; desperate or anxious to speak perhaps, but held back by the finer points of an oppressive etiquette; or obliged to ignore us, to hesitate, wink, or just be silly. And one should not forget how different from the living are they who have passed through death's customs house, which should be understood as a passageway, a funnel, with steps ascending or descending, an explosion, an unravelling. One must ponder too the technical difficulties, linguistic impediments, complications with respect to suitable and unsuitable times and places, the demands, both proper and unreasonable; and finally, the hermeneutics of their response.

Nevertheless, it is always possible to find someone eager to strike his skull against death's barricade, and this research continues and is even gaining in academic respectability and scientific rigour; all this despite the fact that its advocates may only aspire to a certain muted splendour and a modest and rather dubious reputation.

The first question then must be: is communicating with the dead permitted? Is it simply just plain rude? Is it wicked? Is it a sin beyond redemption? Is it an unpardonable discourtesy?

It is well known that religions are generally opposed to this kind of communication; they allude to impiety, refer to prohibitions from Heaven or Hell, or lay down elaborate, insuperable barriers. But the real reason for this prohibition can be explained quite differently. And that is because — one may whisper it with some boldness — religions, like mazes made of mushrooms or architecture from bean soup, are very resistant to the idea of research being conducted in areas where it is likely that any discoveries may turn out to be very difficult to confirm or approve once they have been put forward. And thus the opinionated ministers of religion advise against it, and grinding their teeth in gentle menace, they snarl and sneer in order to dissuade the inquisitive faithful from lifting the skirts of the transcendental, which they wish to remain very long and all-enfolding. Others suppose that their overwhelming fear concerns what might follow from this, namely an alliance of the living with the dead which may well undermine their long-standing dominion over earthly souls. An alternative view can be acknowledged; it appears both strange and questionable that those who take no cognisance of eternal decrees of any other kind are rigorous and orthodox solely in respect of those which are concerned with the dialogue with the dead. And further, such theological prohibitions appear to be devices suggested more by hesitancy and fox-like caution than by true holiness or heartfelt anxiety.

Some other well-educated experts, however, will no doubt raise further well-argued objections. Call up the dead if you wish, they say, but this will only have the effect of discomposing and vexing them as they slumber in their cocoon of shadow; of stirring them from a sleep whose depths and therapeutic properties we can never understand; and if being pestered by telephones and doorbells is an unbearable discourtesy, how crass would it be to act in such a way that necessitates tampering with the very curtains of the great over-arching sky and the bed-linen of eternity, and shattering the silence and profoundly disturbing these defenceless phantoms?

One could counter: "That the dead fall asleep is either a metaphor or it is to be taken literally. In the first instance it is presumed that death may not be sleep exactly, and any exceptions raised by a literal reading will fail because the language used is figurative. If on the other hand we were willing to allow that it *is* sleep, exactly that, then certain bizarre and beautiful consequences arise. Because, if they sleep, they also dream. And what are their dreams? Nightmares? Epiphanies? Or do they dream their own death, perhaps? And if they do not dream, it will be quite sufficient to say that this is not exactly sleeping. In which case, might it not be the moment to throw them off balance so that they stretch out a hand to us? We, with our candles and flowers and pilgrimages and canticles and words of blessing and moving on tiptoe as we whisper with a finger to our lips — which we then raise up to the Ceiling Most High, or, falling headlong, to the Lowest Floor — so as not to disturb them, the immortal ones! But will the dead not simply ignore us with a yawn, or a half-hearted entreaty?"

Others will advise against this out of a "love of decency", as they call it, a kind of indifference that is partly arrogant, partly bigoted: "To have truck with the dead is like displaying one's posterior in public — or one's private parts; because the dead participate in the personal, the deeply essential; and it is not for nothing that they retreat to the bowels of the earth, and settle in its inner organs like faeces or secret tumours; and it is not by chance that, as many have related, they appear in dreams, which reek of pillows damp with perspiration and the body's nocturnal rumbling. It seems indeed that a certain lack of modesty, or at least indecency, may be integral to the character of the dead; and that in their world, be it down below or up above, there may be no place for polite and graceful conversation, for the refinements of courtesy, no space at all for decent clothes; but that instead all is nakedness and cries of pain and entreaties, of pushing and shoving, slavish piety and arrogant display."

Many are doubtful as to the propriety of violating the barrier between the living and the dead; they judge it to be as appropriate as the separation between men and women in public baths; and they hold the opinion that the foul cesspit of the universe has, in addition to the two traditional exits, one other, and over it is written the words "The Dead", and that it opens out on to an internal corridor, which leads to further barriers, open spaces, passages and vestibules dedicated to a variety of punishments and delights.

Finally we will briefly examine the circumspections and objections of modern scholars. Their views do not originate, self-evidently, in epiphanies or from authoritative announcements which address matters of this nature, but rather in shrewd and subtle arguments wherein the breadth of their gaze is wedded to the minutiae of highly specific debate. All these scholars are humanists, which is to say that, in their different ways, they present themselves as being deeply concerned with the human condition, and therefore declare themselves hostile to death, and judge death as either ideologically reprehensible or reactionary, or as a simple technical problem that can be resolved by appropriate methods, or even as a form of anti-social sabotage. We might add, furthermore, that they consider death to be alien and incompatible to man, and are bored with the actual dead themselves, although some see them as allies, others as somewhat guilty underdogs, or as those overtaken by their own worthlessness, or even as the hired killers of a mindless power.

Some of them say: "The dead are set apart from history, *ergo*, apart from art and morality; they have no knowledge of dialectics, and perhaps lack any language. Untouched by any moral scruples they are dysfunctional, uneducated, even perverse." Others believe that "those who are now dead did not, even when alive, inhabit history; rather it was prehistory, something beyond reason, irrational, superstitious and savage. Therefore the dead are not, and cannot possibly be, other than behind the times. As for dallying in retrospective repartee with them, might they not be victims or murderers, and thus delay, even if only for a moment, the forward progress of History?" They may add: "We assume the language of the dead cannot have for its object anything but the dead themselves; therefore, it cannot be understood, and so we judge it to be meaningless."

Others again have suggested a preliminary interview with the dead person invited to engage in dialogue; or they have proposed complex strategies by way of guarantees; or that they be required to prepare for tests which will ascertain the dead person's reliability and cultural awareness. But this circumspection, partly diffident and partly inimical, takes us beyond the problem of simple legitimacy, and leads us towards a different kind of debate.

II.

It has even been argued in some quarters that this particular discussion should be abandoned, not because of the intrinsic illegitimacy of the proposition or any divine ordinance, but because the actual behaviour of the dead inclines one to the belief that pursuing it will be a waste of time and effort — like trying to straighten dogs' legs — which the dead will find in every way distressing; and that in fact all this prevarication, reticence and excess of circumlocution does not arise from objective difficulties but from inherent baseness, from the ill-mannered loutishness, carelessness and arrogance of the dead. In the past a doctrine based upon this view was in fact elaborated by one scholar of the deceased and their ways, and was adopted by a sect whose history is here briefly sketched out.

A History of the Anti-Mortalists

There was, for the time it lasted, a proud and factious sect composed of men who were both melancholy and deeply strange. This sect was founded by an apostate monk of whom legend has it that during his lifetime he sought to make contact with the dead in a variety of ways, obtaining results that were at once so ridiculous, or rather provocative, that in the end he developed an extremely violent antipathy towards the deceased, which gradually increased in its contempt, hatred, madness and wild anger. And from this anger or fury he developed a doctrine which we venture to summarise as follows:

1) Dying is immoral: in dying, a person tears up the living syntax of human conversation, withdraws himself from the collective commitment to feelings and obligations, and becomes an outlaw, a fugitive outside all human compliance;

2) The dead man, therefore, is an outsider, a thug, a rascal; this is demonstrated by the wicked deeds of ghosts, who are no more than criminals, smashers-of-streetlights and violators-of-grandmothers;

3) The dead man raves in silence not because he cannot do anything else but because he is ridiculing our deepest desires; he deceives us, battles against us and frustrates us; he laughs at us; the dead — so the monk insisted — consider their death to be some sort of qualification or a chivalric title, and, haughty and boorish, treat the living like schoolchildren immersed in their revision notes for the imminent agony of death;

4) In conclusion, he proposed to repay the dead with insults and rebukes of every kind. Desecrate them, besmirch their corpses, he proclaimed; to the dogs with them, to the dogs; in graveyards, latrines and brothels and on their headstones: abominations and obscenities.

There was something at once heroic and desperate in this proclamation, and for some time the sect enjoyed the quiet acclaim of thinking persons. Then even those who loathed death took up dying; and no recall to the commitments of the doctrine, no warnings seemed capable of dissuading them from taking a step so serious that it was, in fact, ideologically irreparable. Thus the suspicion dawned on their contemporaries that some among them were acting in bad faith, and while incorruptible in what they professed, were in fact absolutely corrupt and even, perhaps, under a mask of opposition, aiding and abetting death and the dead; and when their leader himself acceded to the forbidden act of death, the murmuring grew into first an outcry and then universal derision. He fought against it as much as he was able, but in the end had to submit, maintaining, however, with more sophistry than honesty, that his demise had been inspired by very significant objectives, namely matters of documentation and research.

With the death of its leader, the most contentious and fanatical of these misguided "deserters", the sect assumed other, more moderate doctrines. They took to deploring death or rather, as they put it — and not without a certain urbane wit — to "counselling against it", for their ideas on the dead were shifting, as will be explained below in the actual words of these followers.

Some amongst them began to assert that the silent haughtiness of the dead did not originate in arrogance or ignorance, but from their becoming, in death, mere idiots. This assertion bore two interpretations, one in truth an act of desperation, the other grounded in greater circumspection.

"Given the current state of our cognisance," one of them observed, "we cannot rule out the possibility that death makes its unfortunate sufferers stupid. And perhaps the atmosphere of the world beyond — the invasiveness of disembodied voices, the loss of limbs, at once invisible and brutal, the ending or disfigurement of their love affairs, the loneliness and sudden contact with new and unknown crowds, perhaps alien and monstrous — precipitates in them a condition of befuddled stupor from which neither prayers nor offerings can rouse them; nor do we know whether a remedy for this horrendous paralysis is ever to be hoped for." Others, with a more thoughtful courtesy towards the dead understood as a group, opined: "If the dead be idiots, as some suppose, and with some justification, the cause may not be the stupefaction of death, which may affect in equal measure all the deceased, but rather our having contacted, up to now, only the idiotic dead. There are two possible reasons for this: in the first place, simple statistics, namely that the majority, let us say almost the totality, of the dead will be only slightly less than completely idiotic, assuming that in the realms of the Afterworld the percentage matches that which pertains in our earthly realm. Alternatively, it could be that the dead arrange themselves in ranks and levels and that the stupid, as a result of their natural gravity, are crowded into the lowest, deepest strata, while the most wise are to be found poised at the very top; and our probes may be clogged up in this plankton of the dead, like nets that are filled up with tiny and inedible small fish while the larger forms, heavy with flesh and with powerful fins, remain at the bottom and glow with a light that is not ours."

Still others surmised, rather subtly: "It is not improbable that the blame for this distressing situation might be attributed to the manifest and laughable self-abasement of the living when confronted with the dead: their devotion, vulnerable to the most childish lies, the remorse with which they gather and celebrate the smallest indication of the presence of one such — the cult of reliquaries, the fraudulence of epigraphs — all this has provoked disgust among the honourable and respectable dead and flattered only the dregs of Hell; unless the dead, deathly pale and weary, are intoxicated by this behaviour to such a degree of foolish excitement that they behave like side-show clowns raised up to the rank of film stars."

Assuming this hypothesis that the dead are fools be true, further ingenious suggestions have been put forward as to why this may be the case. There are some who wish, as with paralytics, to re-educate those amongst the dead who have been terrified by death by enticing them with treats and trivia: luxurious and flattering liturgies, tombstones and libations, devotional dances. In this way they hope that the dead will understand that, when they come face to face with the living, and are able to disentangle themselves from their ruinous stupor, then much greater rewards than such baubles will ensue. Certain others propose — and it is a risky idea — to train those of the young who are marked out by their great mettle and clarity of mind, so that they become experts in death and are thus prepared for their own dying; and once they attain adulthood, to dispatch them painlessly, so that these pioneers may forge a bridgehead in the undiscovered country; and there make contact with various classes of the dead, identifying the best and greatest, until finally these logical and laical psychopomps shall conduct them forth to converse with the living.

Yet others of this sect, with greater courtesy, have suggested that the dead are not so much stupid and hostile, as deaf. In their opinion death is an ear-shattering yet inaudible explosion which causes irreparable damage to the hearing; consequently, these persons, dwelling in places they suppose to be totally padded, do not notice our voices and perhaps do not even suspect their existence. There are, finally, some who imagine that the dead may in fact be frozen and rendered insensible by the cold spaces in which they dwell; they propose, as a preliminary measure to some sort of attempt at conversation, to warm up their abodes with heat-generating rockets.

And there is one commentator who firmly believes that the reticence of the dead does not originate in clumsiness, arrogant reluctance or unfortunate deafness, but in wearisome impotence, extraneous impediments, fraud or surreptitious bullying. This is not the place, however, to discuss by whom this is all arranged or how it is endured.

III.

Up to this point we have considered the objections which preclude conversations with the dead, put forward by those who hold that it is either not permitted or is useless, given that those who have passed on are stupid or deaf or louts.

Other scholars, however, have set to one side such value judgements and supposed that the problem of thanato-communication is a purely technical issue, a matter of opening up roads and trying out new routes, and relying on the fact that some sort of way forward will doubtless turn up. They throw themselves into this work, thinking up devices that will achieve this aim, so that the dead, in finding themselves besieged so ingeniously, thereby acquaint themselves with the notion of conversing with the living.

In order to treat the problem with absolute scientific rigour, certain preliminary questions need to be asked; and in considering these, namely the places in which the dead exist, or the forms they assume, or the languages they speak, we will briefly examine the conclusions in the order given above.

As to where the dead exist, complaints abound: "This mortifying elusiveness on the part of the dead in regard to their place of residence, which is generally held to be 'up above' or 'down below' as if they were deeply afraid of intrusive and tactless questioners, or querulous beggars…" It has even been assumed that this reticence, so the argument goes, is because the Beyond is a region of ill-repute, a vile place, a huge bachelor pad, somewhere secret, albeit as vast as the universe, and a stage for wild though incorporeal debaucheries.

One may skim through the following testimonial: "When I put this problem to myself in the first instance — many years ago now — I undertook to investigate what dwelling-place the dead had chosen, or had been sent to, supposing that they might dwell somewhere well protected but nevertheless accessible, for otherwise every effort would be in vain, and our hard work would be to no avail. Going over in my mind certain old tales, I imagined their world to be very close to ours, but sharply confined, a narrow space that would certainly be an effective hiding-place, for who could adequately investigate all the places found in this world of ours that are constructed in such a way?" The account goes on to say, with a rather verbose punctiliousness, how a web of informers spread out to different places — perhaps they were more accomplices than what you might call fellow conspirators — all focused on the unearthing of some clue that would eventually, so to speak, reveal the epicentres of the world of the dead.

"One evening last winter," we resume, citing this strange text, "I received from my friend, removed to a point of vantage in a rural area, a message as exciting as it was outlandish; he had found a thing so strange it beggared belief. Pitting the dog days of my madness against the cold ungrateful night, I pluck up courage and in the light off the snow race through the blackness of the night; I reach my friend and find him wide awake, all agog. In a frenzy he flings me into an old outhouse where a few farm tools are hanging; he hands me something, picked up heaven knows where, a cold metal hexagon, a cell from a mechanical honeycomb. A rusted and worn-out countersink nursed unloved in its lap a small screw-head; he signals to me that I should put it to my ear. I comply, and listen; a faint murmur and a cry of grief, a gasp, tiny but none the less human. I am afraid, I tremble, I experience the extremes of delirious exhaustion. Is this, then, the dwelling-place of the dead? Are the dead so slight as to be able to reside in so small a space? Or were they shielded by some ingenious invisibility? Perhaps they were lodged, elbow to elbow, along the ridges of this infinitely small funnel? We hear shouts mingled with groans, cries for help, perhaps, and reproaches. Was this the mournful kingdom of the damned? Or a colony isolated from their motherland? And — a new and unsettling question — how long had this 'thing' existed? No more than ten years. So did the nether regions relocate themselves? Or was this a recently set-up outpost, a satellite for the newly dead, murderers whose death had not yet been sifted out from the others, suicides whose death no other death can ever exonerate?

"After half an hour or so, the countersink falls silent. Oh well: so they have migrated to another locale. Where to? Can we follow them? Where are they housed, wearing what kinds of clothing, in what artificial hiding-place, these untrustworthy, elusive dead? I despair of ever finding myself again so close to knowing. And this concern to understand turns into a desperate yearning, a numb, devastating anxiety which ages me at a stroke, as if I am rushing to meet someone at a crossroads that is familiar to me alone.

"Some time ago I began carefully to examine empty mine-shafts, and might well have found one which went down into the lowest depths; I beat the walls with a stick: those shafts that echo with a sound of emptiness I search. I strike fear into lizards and snakes. I watch the creatures dart away across the ground and wonder: might the kingdom of the dead be contained in a lizard's rotten tooth, in a snake's egg, or even hang from the retina of a sewer rat?"

"If the dead are nomadic," another researcher writes, "we would need to position instruments designed to capture them as they move with all their belongings from one dwelling-place to another; small sticky nets, for example, should be stretched across their temporary resting-places, so that they find themselves entangled in the act of flight." Another researcher retorts: "If the dead are something watery or airy, which glues would work? Can whirlwinds or water sprites be ensnared?"

Elsewhere we read: "From certain ramblings of his father when on the point of death, a friend has come to believe that the dead are subjected to compression, like flour; that is, they are kneaded together with certain empyrean waters, whisked up into lightness, cooked in the perfect radiance that pertains up above, and then spread out across the open spaces of the sky, rather like sheets of pasta. He maintains that the Earth's dead form a continuous focaccia, that, beyond the vicinity of the moon, expands into space as far as Mars, which, however, it does not quite reach. This material, if crumbled, finely milled, carefully liquidised and thoroughly boiled with the puffs of heavenly air contained within, is suitable for empyrean stomachs (if such there are), or rather, he adds, that the end of the world will be marked by a delicious funeral banquet, in which the holiest of diners will feast on this very focaccia. And so why not send into this region of the sky probes made of some spongy prehensile material capable of indicating to us where on their journey the dead were made into flour? What could better assuage our incessant hunger than a mouthful of *focaccia suprême?*

Sundry researchers, convinced that the kingdom of the dead must be extremely small, record that they had narrowed it down to places usually considered strange and improbable: an old abandoned timepiece, a rust-bound lock, a useless pencil-sharpener. One, noticing the frequency with which mechanical devices were put forward as the possible dwelling-places of the dead, imagined that the complexities of these machines were inherently suited to supporting the remarkably well-organised disposition of the differing hierarchies of those who have passed away. In every way these hypothetical contacts were always ephemeral; in short, the dead — because they had been discovered, or in consequence of some inner unease, either from their own free choice or after being put under duress — removed themselves, and all trace of them was lost. One may also read, by way of commentary, the following testimony: "I am sure that, for no less than eighteen minutes, I discovered the dwelling of the dead, in an old padlock or mortise, a place by no means glamorous, but in fact thought appropriate by one with a greater authority than us who concerns himself with issues of this nature; a padlock, as I was saying, clogged with rust — which had been left quite unused for some time and was hanging on the door of the attic with its shank on the fastening. One morning, finding myself close by and just for something to do, partly from domestic necessity, partly as a sop to my fancy of finding the dead, and imagining that this messy mixture of things unfinished and undone might well be enticing to the dead in search of somewhere to settle, I noticed, while moving this lock, that it emitted a completely unexpected squeak that resembled a cry of derision as if it were scoffing at me, but without scorn; and at the same time a wail of grief as if suffering a punishment, or as a prayer for forgiveness, as if to say in the same breath, 'Fool, can't you see?' and 'Why do you ignore me?' Well versed in the shifting, fleeting character of these dwelling-places, I refrained from showing any surprise, fear or interest. Rather, the better to gloss over my sagacity, I said in a normal voice — for the dead are not, as some imagine, a little hard of hearing — 'This lock could do with a spot of oil,' and looking to one side I made a show of busying myself with something else. Well then, as soon as I passed nearby again I heard renewed groans and cries of grief that had a certain rhythmic quality, like psalms or snatches of the litany; I moved closer, and maintaining my lackadaisical manner went through the motions of raising the latch. Raising the latch of the Universe! Within it lay the past life of the world, and all of its sins perhaps. I put my ear to the tiny aperture and listened: and from within there came a confused and breathless anguish of voices all mixed together, deafening me with whistlings, sarcastic laughter, gurglings, gobblings, retchings, garbled syllables, fragments of defunct and corrupted dictionaries perhaps, the ashes of cadaverous grammars raised up to a state of extreme turbulence by a catastrophic miniature hurricane; and then I shouted into the lock, 'Who are you?' and asked further questions, as loudly as I could but the groaning did not modulate, nor yet answer me. Eventually the din of voices calmed down and after a little more than fifteen minutes it fell completely silent. And when I wanted to raise the lock, now voiceless, I found it as light as ever in my hand; carefully I took it to pieces, but found nothing inside apart from the dirty fragments of its mechanism, its rust and dust. I wondered whether they had heard my voice; and if, had they heard it, they thought it unfriendly, or whether, quite simply, they did not understand what I was saying."

In relation to these lines of research, the following observation has been made: "Who can assure us that in locks, in broken clocks, in drawers and crowded attics, it was only the dead, organised in their otherworldly realms, who were granted hospitality? Others looking for places in which to dwell might overrun these same spaces: vagabond types, demi-hooligans, phantasms with nowhere to rest, along with those less than dead, failures in death, who have been cast out from the rightful regions of the deceased. And might this perhaps explain their choice of such poor and inappropriate dwelling-places? Might it not be that for them these places resemble what here below would be park-benches, or a spot underneath the arches? And these meaningless hullabaloos, do they not resemble the gibberings of drunkards, the guffaws of trouble-makers?"

NOTE

Vagabond types, or perennials: Since they have never been born, "perennials" never die, but despite never experiencing death one would hesitate to call them immortal. One may consider their death to be in a continual state of reinvigoration, or, by means of a theocratic fiction, it can be supposed to have already occurred. Feline and thoroughly wicked, they are overwhelmingly wretched; they have no purpose whatsoever. They take on a variety of forms but their special quality originates in their always leaning at an angle, and for this reason they constantly slide about, although their descent towards the depths of bottomless abysses appears to be over quickly and does them no great harm. It is said that every few centuries a conference is called in these abysses with the aim of resolving the nagging problem of perennials; but the meetings are inconclusive, and these tattered souls survive. Their origin is obscure; their temperament unpleasant; their fate ill-fortuned, as if they were always on the point of dying but will never do so.

Demi-hooligans: Foci of evil and wickedness, and at the same time, immaturity; in the views of some, souls of the aborted: a metaphor that indicates the impression they convey of an innate lack of emotion; they enter into the world — what world? — from the womb of night, along with certain baleful birth fluids, and they can best be described as concentrations of teeth and freckles. The maternal sense of the comets, so they say, might be called on to persuade them to take care of these unruly children; whether that be merely a fable I really do not know, but there is much that could be said regarding the feminine qualities of all these long-hairs excepting that it does not touch upon the subject of this disquisition.

Phantasms: Loose wefts of faltering syntax stretched across the sky like advertisements or political slogans; infinitely decomposable and recomposable; with rudimentary eyes placed haphazardly, they show a tendency towards groundless, or at least inelegant obsessions. Harmless, if a trifle disgusting, because of their unpleasantness and moral bankruptcy; often referred to as things of pulp and as the rubbish of the universe.

Failed and unhoused dead: According to those who are not among the least well-informed, dying is not a process that brings closure, but is a mere preliminary, and the quality of "being dead" is not a natural state, but a heraldic decoration, an honour, an award of merit. To die is nothing more than completing the application for admission to classes which are a preparation for dying. Those recently deceased are committed, by a series of requirements, to familiarising themselves with specific topics, to engage in rituals, and to abstain from visiting certain individuals.

Rejected applicants are shut out by the gates of the underworld and some prostrate themselves in grief outside; others just roam about, some return to stroll around among the living. Tittering, untrustworthy, these Lumpendead often cause a rumpus at the gates of the Empyrean; once dispersed, they move on to gang up with more foolish phantasms, whom they corrupt; otherwise they supply the long-living with second-hand ideologies, and childish demi-hooligans with forged visas.

IV.

There are many who remain convinced that the profound difficulty involved with communicating with the dead derives not from their being already settled in places that defy prediction, in sealed-off and voiceless locations, but, on the contrary, from their lack of a defined domicile or of having one with unprecedented dimensions.

It has been stated categorically that: "The dead are not concentrated in places allocated for the purpose, but are either distributed across the entire universe at random according to their own convenience, or as the winds, as it is said, rush through space and buffet them. And if the Earth, as seems quite probable, is the only place where life flourishes — its ripeness beyond all imagining, its putrefaction the noblest, its self-knowledge feeble — and is dedicated to the production of the dead, then imagine if things were otherwise: what a density of the dead would be spread throughout the cosmos when a few dozen deceased among the stellar systems already feels like unbearable overcrowding, and what would be the probability of colliding with one of them if in our own solar system there were ten, or a hundred, or even a thousand of them? And so what is the likelihood of our ever finding any of the dead of a special moral or intellectual character, with whom one could consider making time for engaging in conversation? And even if there be life rooted elsewhere which is capable of ripening into death, what pleasure would we take in that? Certainly then our atmosphere here would swarm with the densest rabble of the dead, though they would lie outside our grasp, incompatible with and isolated from us by virtue of their language, their habits and desires; and then perhaps the labour of searching among so many different dead, in order to gather the rarest and most widely scattered of our ancestors, would become ever more desperate."

Pursuing a rather different line, it has been stated elsewhere that: "It is not impossible that the dead that are closely related to us concentrate in nearby areas, but not, as outlined above, exactly neighbouring on our world. The metaphor of 'Heaven' and 'Hell' in everyday poetic language strove to convey precisely that meaning: that the location of the dead is not so much distant from us as detached from our world. What goes on there will not be a matter of intrepid missions, imaginative forays or shoulders set against bronze gates, but of dark stratagems, fantastical or deceptively casual approaches and perhaps even forged papers or disguises.

"Supposing that at the end of their melancholy voyage — a wandering journey, both overwhelmingly burdensome and tortuous, as the ancient Baedekers of the underworld inform us — the dead were to be found encamped across huge fields, or in scattered villas, or cities, protected by terrorist mountain ranges and didactic woods, metaphors of towers and gateways; guarded by allegorical beasts, like Silence, motionless and full of fury, or by chaste, cold Distance and patient Desolation, by Angels and Demons too, those sergeants and bureaucrats of the abyss; then, unless we were able to mask ourselves with all the strategies of Nothingness, who would dare to set foot in this Tibet of Non-being?"

But we also read: "Anyone who believes the dead to be hard of hearing must regard death to be a sort of explosion capable of rendering the deceased stone-deaf, so that communicating with them becomes not only extremely difficult but difficult to a ridiculous degree, meaningless and absurd. We have come to the conclusion that dying may indeed be an explosive gateway of fire that leads to the empyrean, which is not peripheral to death but rather its familiar. In this way then, the dead, in the act of dying, are dispersed to an incredible degree, and on that basis too are they undone and made insubstantial. In these circumstances the real difficulty may lie in their being of disproportionate dimensions, thinly spread and gaseous, and yet as enormous as continents, asteroids or planets. And here one cannot avoid touching on certain interrelated problems: whether rarefaction to this extent may assist the dead in co-existing in the same space with a great number of their fellows by exercising a scrupulous differentiation amongst themselves; or if, on the contrary, the pneumatic properties of the dead do not in fact force them to distance themselves greatly from one another, so that they are able to slide with ease over each other and bounce like rubber from place to place."

Followers in a variety of disciplines have proposed devising some form of condenser which would be able to bring together a greater part of the dead on Earth by solidifying or making substantial those that already wander over it. Some of them suppose that the dead can be gathered together by a circular motion, a little like a whirlpool; others dream of a magnet, a sort of motionless motor around which the rennet of the hovering dead would coagulate, or to which their favus would cling. Another scientist wishes to cast huge nets across the skies, rather like bird snares, in the hope of netting flocks of filleted dead, in order to gather and knit them together again; there are others again who imagine using plumes of exhalations from the very finest viscous froth, certain that by this means fragments of the feathery dead would be captured, sufficient to reconstruct one and coerce it into conversation, once it had been brought to ground.

V.

To those who maintain that the dimensions of the dead are such that it is necessary to perform a preliminary process of condensation or coagulation upon them, the following objection has been raised: "For have we not come to the conclusion that where the dead are of a substantial size then some evidence of their presence would have been picked up by our instruments? We believe, on the contrary, that the difficulty of locating the dead is more likely in consequence of their being extremely small. No larger than fragments of bacteria — so that all the dead of the Roman Empire might be chained to the whirligig of an electron. In which case, what instruments can we use to address this problem of communicating with the dead?" An answer then follows: "We have constructed certain voice-reducers, whose purpose is to recreate human speech, but precisely miniaturised. Having formulated elementary phrases in both living and dead languages, the sound of voices recorded and compressed in this way was broadcast to a large number of very small sites, the *topoi*, and at each *topos* a sophisticated amplifier designed for the purpose was employed to reconstitute the recorded sounds; the death-rattle of a bacterium in agony became the deafening howl of a klaxon, and the gaseous rumblings of digestive cells resembled the roar of a volcano. That the results were poor should not surprise us, seeing that the *topoi* are potentially infinite; however, a group of our researchers seems recently to have received, as a response from one of these *topoi*, a brisk homily, something like *haklut* or *haglut* with the 'h' aspirated, an obscure word certainly, from a language not known to the living perhaps, and lost in the passage of time, or maybe, as others have suggested, a proper name. Successive phonic stimuli directed at the same site have failed to attract any further response, except possibly a short sound suggestive of mockery, although that seems hard to believe."

Other researchers, inclined to believe in the microscopic exiguity of the dead, suggest a different approach: "Instead of dragging the whole contraption from one place to another, why not create artificially a *megatopos* by amalgamating a number of *topoi*? The probability of our encountering one of the dead in an active *topos* would thereby be considerably increased." To which came the reply: "We are not sure whether the harassment experienced by the dead in such a process of concentration would not disturb, alienate or disorient them in unsuspected ways. No procedure of this nature should be permitted unless it carries the basic guarantee that it causes no harm to the deceased." With greater audacity, or perhaps simple thoughtlessness, the following argument was proposed: "This similarity between the dead and bacteria opens up another way of addressing the question and perhaps of bringing it to a close. It could be that advantageous conditions exist that would be particularly conducive to the well-being of those who have passed on: easily digestible food, pleasantly warm accommodation and congenial relationships. Why not create such an ambience in the lab? In other words, prepare a culture of the dead in a test tube. And if we could discover some kind of gelatine that is particularly nourishing and in which they might sustain themselves, then we should be able to undertake a pioneering laboratory study and subject them to experiments as frequently as may be necessary, and so eventually bend them, these eternally unruly, to engage in sustained and sensible dialogue."

And for those inclined to doubt the wisdom of this, considering that the treatment of the dead requires from experimenters all the will-power and energy they are able to muster, the robust response is that bacteria are no less virulent and quarrelsome in test-tube conditions than they are in human blood and that such treatment will in the end certainly benefit the dead themselves by releasing them from their melancholy wandering through cold and inhospitable space. And this despite there being many who do not shrink from referring to the "uncivilised nature" of the deceased, even when they are located in comfortable surroundings specifically designed for socially valuable activities. To those wondering what sort of experiments might be performed upon the dead in such caring circumstances, the obvious response would be:

"Moral experiments: what reaction the dead have to good or evil; whether they experience reciprocal affection, jealousies or suspicions; whether they are misanthropists or philanthropists; whether they are pranksters or hypochondriacs; whether they are to be suspected of employing the evil eye or witchcraft or are specially skilled in the rituals of exorcism; whether they are endogamous or exogamous, whether, in other words, they mate with the dead from other constellations; or alternatively are compelled to procreate with their compatriots; or possibly that they have neither sexual relations nor progeny. Scientific experiments: whether they undergo any form of evolution; whether they are effective conductors of electricity; finally, whether they die, and if it is possible, in such a situation, to kill them. This last 'experiment' would open the way to the verification of another suggestion: that not only is our death their birth, which is perfectly obvious, but that their death is our birth. In all cases these experiments will assist in the recovery of our ancestors, whom we will be able to enclose in tiny portable containers; and these cylinders, packed with the dead, from our contemporaries all the way back to the Neanderthals, will constitute both the most appropriate escutcheon for our times and an inexhaustible storehouse of our past, from which, thanks to the favourable conditioning of the dead, we will be able to draw endless information, curious facts and insights."

This notion of making the dead "squeal" through recourse to all manner of abuses and scientific tortures — with perfectly well-understood threats rather than imaginary ones — has provoked reaction both from religious figures and humanists, who have denounced what they describe as "plots hatched by today's dead against the deceased of yesteryear". The responses to this statement, reminiscent of a certain amount of anti-scientific odium, have asserted that, with the dead, as with other stubborn rebels and reluctant recidivists, everything was permissible, even indeed to act at the extreme limits of power; and if they were able to maintain their silence under a torturer from the world beyond, other torturers would learn from them; and in the end, torn between contrary terrors, some would submit. Adding to this scientism a pedantic cruelty that smacks of fascism, a cry of command, half furious, half blasphemous, has been uttered: "Colonise the dead!" There are those who wish to subdue the dead by force, to domesticate them, indoctrinate them and inure them like slaves to tasks and activities denied to men of flesh: interplanetary espionage, centuries–long voyages through the cosmos, exploratory journeys into the abyss, manœuvres deep underground.

Finally, there are some who consider that such abuses of the deceased, having provoked in them defensive actions, and compelling them perhaps into organising themselves, might give rise to a universal dialectic between this world and the other, one destined to make everything anew, which would offer grounds for hope of an innovative de-theocratisation of space, and in turn for mutual assemblies, public gatherings, elections and debates, with no conditions imposed on either side, to be followed by binding decrees. And perhaps — for thus does this irrepressible ideologue, this fantastical prophet of revolutionary change, bring his argument to an end — from this, the final day will dawn whereupon the Senate of the Living and of the Dead, voting unanimously upon a common motion, will force the President of the Immortals into the minority.

VI.

We must also make reference, out of a love for comprehensiveness, to other learned theories, which present differing degrees of validity. For instance, that the dead may be very thin and attenuated: according to some scholars up to three or four kilometres long, and according to others, thousands upon thousands of kilometres; and that because of this they extend well beyond the borders of the Earth's atmosphere. If the first description holds true, perhaps it will not be impossible to use the dead a little like antennae; in the latter case, one might hope to entangle them in cables cast from orbiting spacecraft.

Other experts judge their form to be spherical, a proclivity that is not innocent of certain philosophical and mathematical preconceptions which appear inimical to scrupulous research. Among those who favour the spherical, there are some who imagine the dead to be quite small balls, which bounce up and down on the ground, while others consider them to be of merely average density and that they float about through space.

Certain prophets of the fantastical believe the dead have their dwelling within the capital letters of illuminated manuscripts, cowering in the heart of these elegant labyrinths when a reader's fingers play upon the book and all their exits sealed between its covers, but, when the book rests in its vertical berth, they roam around, and go visiting. This is a theory which regards the dead as purposefully obstructive, that in fact they live in a condition of majestic, if slightly ironical indolence.

Those who suppose that the dead reside within sounds see the problem in a rather similar manner, if somewhat aesthetically; as soon as the deceased hear anything, be it the sound of a voice or an instrument, they seize upon it immediately, slipping themselves inside, just like an acrobat seizing the trapeze flying ahead of him, and no sooner does the phonic foothold float away than they glide across to another, and it is there that they dwell, moving further and further on; and for this reason our world is completely embroidered with the dead who spring from sound to sound; and this, some suppose, can be seen as an explanation of rhythm, which gracefully controls the entire ensemble of moans and roars, arias and crashes; and thus the dead create among the things of our world a movement like a thread which stitches, binds and holds all together.

Some observers imagine they see this weaver's shuttle within drops of rain, and that heavy showers would be nothing but shoals of the dead within which we walk, dense to a greater or lesser degree, according to whether it is only drizzling or pelting down. They believe that the falling drops produce a murmuring or a rumble resembling words, scarcely articulated or spoken chorally, which can only come from the dead within. They have also put forward as evidence certain recordings, although these seem more evocative than convincing.

Another group favours snow, and sees the dead in its delicate crystals, intricate small chambers and undefiled sarcophagi; but if this were the case the living would only have dealings with the dead in the winter. And that does not seem at all likely.

VII.

Now, moving towards the conclusion of our disquisition, we must confront a problem so recondite and unrewarding that it leaves us doubting whether we can ever bring this study to a close. This problem being: what language do the dead speak?

Namely, if Language has an intimate relationship with the world, or rather, as some would prefer, is the world itself, does it not seem reasonable to believe that the other universe desires, or requires, or is its very own language? Additionally, death may be nothing more than a translating machine, which overturns and makes new our grammar, syntax and vocabulary; or rather, that it is only death which can convey us from one morphological system to another.

That is to say, those who believe that the dead, in the world beyond, may continue speaking their language from this earthly world, fail to bear in mind that there, the languages of this Earth, whatever they may be, would be unable to provide any basis for the discussion of the objects, actions and conceptions particular to that place. So a new language will be obligatory. Some suppose it to be entirely new; others favour an antique language, though enhanced in order to deal with its new tasks. But against these latter, an objection arises: "The dead, if not separated by nationhood or language — which appears unlikely — will either be isolated, and thus stripped of any means of discourse whatsoever, or be gathered together in various ways and thus be in communion each with another; and in such a case a new language will be doubly necessary, both because of the novelty of their surroundings and in order to assimilate the discourse of the deceased of differing nationalities; hence it seems wise to consider that they will have a new language appropriate to this existence and which all regard as their own; it will have a different character from any possible language in this world, and will be in every way unintelligible to us."

These concerns — which it seems rash to dismiss as being without foundation, developed as they were, in a time gone by, in a slim volume not altogether devoid of theoretical excellence — threw the massed ranks of the scholars of mortality into despondent disarray; a few, convinced but still daunted, abandoned their research; others, convinced but undeterred, strove to explore whether it was at all possible to unearth this putative language of the dead; given that the attractiveness of such a proposition would mean that this language, once discovered, would facilitate discourse with the dead of all nations and of every age.

Those dedicated to the collection and cataloguing of all non-human sounds and noises, from whatever source — and all the better if they be blurred and muddled

— imagined in fact that the vocabulary and interjections of the language of the dead might be found mingled with all the countless noises of the everyday, from which they proceeded to separate them out and isolate them. Their concept was to organise these sounds according to the various ways they combined and intermingled; and by this process they hoped to draw together an elementary phonetic morphology and then proceed towards a comprehensive syntax. At that point they intended to annotate every single instance in which any sound had been evidenced, with the aim of uncovering permanent relationships between sounds and situations, which they imagined would be signifiers. They succeeded in gathering certain rustlings and clicks, which, through their frequency and perhaps not merely contingent association, it seemed reasonable to suppose were evidence of language. But they could not progress any further, for their procedure suffered a problem, a setback at the very point they had considered to be their most subtle inspiration; for they did not manage to ascertain, nor were they capable of ever understanding, what the situations they should describe might be; and so despite taking notes and cataloguing and revisiting on every occasion their criteria and methods, they ended up in despair, and sometimes even with damaged personal relationships. And it should be added that, however carefully they listened, the sounds discovered seemed rather poorly articulated and somewhat limited as a basis from which to create a language for so significant a dialogue.

With regard to the belief that research into the language of those who have died was fraught with difficulties and impediments, some scholars have considered simply skirting these obstacles: "If, lacking parallel texts or other means of interpretation, we cannot recover the language of the deceased, we could at least attempt to invent such a language ourselves, and then teach it to the dead. Consequently we have adopted the following method: out in the countryside at night, in a silent place as close as possible to a graveyard, picturesque with ruins, we set up a loudspeaker, a projector and a screen; skulls, bones and other such symbols liberally distributed should provide a wink, a nod or a prod as if to say to the dead: 'Look, we're talking to you.' Simple and clearly defined images were then projected on to the screen, and the loudspeaker broadcast its sounds deep into the shadows in every direction, sounds absolutely unambiguous and at the same time rudimentary. The project continued for several weeks and was repeated a number of times. But when finally, after the projector had been switched off, and we broadcast some simple questions into the night and then listened with ears pricked, it was all to no avail. We turned up the sensitivity on the recorder's microphones, again to no avail: rustlings of grass, flights of insects, mutterings of frogs and serpents, but not a single syllable came in reply."

These scholars had thus invented a kind of Esperanto or Volapük for the dead; but it was hard to find anyone who did not see through the sheer foolhardiness and presumption of their endeavours, for they had assumed precisely what was in fact so overwhelmingly unsound: that the dead were inclined to cooperation, ignoring the question of whether they were willing to cooperate, or whether indeed they had the means to comply. This project of a spurious and pointless language, conducted by moonlight out in the fields and graveyards, was more a case of being seduced than of being scrupulous. Nor was there any lack of those who, in jest, suggested that in repeating such a procedure, one should not forget to hold a daily roll-call, in order to establish who among the dead were the most conscientious; and perhaps some sort of transport should be organised, a sleeper wagon to pick up the (deceased) pupils, with their satchels and textbooks, and take them back to their circles in the heavens. In this flawed and probably imprudent experiment some found the proof of what many had suspected: that the dead are arsewipes, slavering simpletons content to sit on their seats, eyes fixed on the screen, listening to the voices and enjoying themselves in the most stupid way, like spectators at a circus; so they learn nothing at all, and have no idea even that there may be something to learn. Such observations perhaps do not aspire to the level of insults, but are more in the way of despairing protestations.

Another ingenious inventor marshalled a range of objections to the experiment described above; he refuted the notion that the linguistic system of the dead — Thanatoglossia, as it might be called, or Avernese — would have recourse to sounds resembling those emitted by our phonatory organs, for the very reasonable reason that the deceased are found lacking in that department. As a consequence, he stated, the lack of response from the dead could be ascribed to the utter impossibility of their articulating proper sounds. Pursuing this particular line of thought, he proposed to devise a system of non-human, non-animal and non-mechanical sounds, imagining these to be more in tune with the senses of those who had passed away. He considered putting at their disposal a user-friendly apparatus, and assembled a device, which he christened a "Defunctaphone", which is briefly described below.

The Defunctaphone is a small box perhaps a metre long, and forty centimetres in height and depth. Into it two hollow jointed pieces of wood are inserted, which are extraordinarily light and are held in place by loosely attached pins; to these pieces of wood are attached, on one side at regular intervals, snippets of bone, cartilage and locks of hair; and on the other side, prongs of distressed wood, razors and fragments of rock; all arranged so that for an element of organic animal material on one side there is a vegetable or mineral element on the other. Resonant sound-boxes and vibratory membranes amplify the sounds; and the creakings, scratchings and murmurings which these throw up bring into being a rich repertoire of modulations sufficient to form the basis of a flexible and quite remarkably expressive language.

In short, the inventor was able to create a series of precise and stable sounds and also to provide a notation for them. He then proceeded to set up his Defunctaphone in locations that appeared particularly apt, graveyards especially, and settings doleful and of fell repute; he waited for one of the deceased to risk using his device, to run their fingers over its keys, which could be easily moved by even the slightest breeze or a child's breath. It may well be that it was this very facility which proved to be the obstacle that hampered the success of his experiment; for the keys often moved on their own accord without any clear intention of making conversation, and if these meaningless oscillations were intermixed with more meaningful sounds, it was simply impossible to distinguish between them.

We would like to bring to the notice of our patient readers the reasons why the inventors of an Esperanto for the dead, or the mastermind behind the Defunctaphone, were minded to set up their instruments in the vicinity of graveyards, and at night. The resort to strategies such as these, the stuff of folklore and poesy, is, one might suppose, condemned by rigorous scientific investigators of the problem, for they judge such a procedure to be mere simple sentimentality, or no more than a literary device. We would, however, be undervaluing such an approach by taking it to be definitively anti-scientific; for it could possibly be a pointer to a new way of conceiving of this research, wherein one might strive, perhaps, to bring together the cool discipline of science with the fervent imaginings of the ancients.

So now we shall bring this little chapter to a close by alluding to an experiment that, since it is still under way, has not yet been exposed to judgement of any kind; except to say that it is certainly the most ambitious and wide-ranging that has so far been envisaged in this field. Various contraptions and devices have been set up to process and record all possible sounds, sonorities and inflexions, and mix them in every imaginable modulation; thunderous at times, at others quietly subdued, they are broadcast into space by rockets and probes, squirted into underground passages and dark secret places, blasted over valleys and mountain peaks, secreted under the earth, deep down into the lowest depths of rivers and oceans; and we hold on to the belief that surrounded by so many sounds, someone among the dead might be confused enough to be provoked into proffering an insult, or voicing an affront, or an entreaty, or perhaps all of these together, inadvertently.

VIII.

This inventory, of grotesque and desperate explorations in search of unbodied ears and mouths without breath, must here reach its conclusion. It will perhaps appear to be no more than a list of unanswered questions. So much invention and sophistry the scornful will say, so much wit, so much artifice, so many contraptions and contrivances; yet what is the reward? Mumbled syllables, a few contemptuous sighs, inarticulate groans; a signage far too meagre to lead us to the city of the dead.

And yet — and yet: who are they, these our monstrous brothers who resemble us but take so different a form? Spheroids, daggers kilometres long, bacteria; jugglers or beasts waiting to ambush a syllable in order, with a single leap, to secrete themselves into our swirl of breath, or to explode across the Earth once more; or are they suspended in regions both calm and unreachable, or reduced to a dispersal of skilfully baked focaccia, the authentic food of the gods? Do they wish to converse with the living? Or are they long-suffering and absent-minded, even a little stupid, or just deaf; or led astray deep into fantasies, in comparison with which earthly madness is but a bank-clerk's abacus? Are they distracted by some loud, vile collective insanity, which prevents them from understanding the voices of the living, or which makes our voices troublesome and hostile to their ecstasies?

One imagines that the dead may be complex and restless, part oppressor, part oppressed, being either hand in glove with officials or opposed to them; compliant or secretly treacherous. That in their homeland, some, half-scheming and half-seditious, will weave together a final revolt, a conflict that will begin with deceptive light-heartedness, but will soon grow in malevolence.

Neither knives nor any other warlike devices are of any use to these unscrupulous conspirators, but only this dialogue, this compact with the living, which they judge to be both subversive and irresistible; for then, as they say with their bitter rhetoric, the sky, like a scrap of newspaper used to wrap up filth, or to wipe one's arse, will be rent from top to bottom. For the sake of this dialogue both charlatans and the scrupulous alike seek out fissures, work underground passages and lairs, scrape away and cut, and insert themselves into these lesions.

Some hint of this dialogue is already in the air, a hilarity at once secret and circumspect, a way of speaking through conspiratorial enigmas.

AFTERWORD

Alastair Brotchie

●

John Walker's Introduction went to great lengths to avoid "spoilers" that might lessen the reader's enjoyment of Manganelli's text. In particular he did not mention something we both became aware of during the translation process, he as translator, I as editor, which would perhaps have been the greatest spoiler of all and which has therefore been relegated to this Afterword instead. While working on this book we noticed many passages that seemed to have a certain arbitrariness, yet far from appearing gratuitous (we became convinced that very little is gratuitous in this book) they appeared to hint at an internal logic whose workings were not immediately evident. One of the great pleasures of preparing this text was our gradual awareness of what this signified, and this should be the reader's pleasure too, so those inclined to read afterwords before the main text may want to stop at this point.

Calvino called the texts in this book "profoundly unified", and we believe that this is very much the case. At the end of his introduction John Walker cites Manganelli's notion of "clarity" whereby meanings are made available beneath or "through" a text, and it is the secondary meaning contained within *To Those Gods Beyond* that we think constitutes the unity attributed to it by Calvino. The essentials of this hidden theme, so to speak, can also be found in Manganelli's manifesto "Literature as Deception". Beneath the gorgeous baroque and gothic surface of *To*

Those Gods Beyond lies an exposition of Manganelli's notion of what literature is, his ideas about the production of literary "objects" and the situation of the manufacturers of such objects. However, the book is of course itself a literary object and so cannot be a simple illustration of the manifesto's propositions. This follows from one of Manganelli's pronouncements (marked by the exaggeration that is deemed essential for manifestos): "the [literary] object born out of the complicity between his ignorance and his knowledge is totally inaccessible to him." Thus for Manganelli the literary object is formed out of a combination of authorial direction and something else which grants it a degree of autonomy and creates a sort of narrative with its own imperatives. As he puts it in "A King":"the eagle, the lion and the serpent, once imagined, did not stop being themselves." It is only occasionally then that the secondary theme becomes visible through the machinations of Manganelli's narrative, before receding back into the depths again but only after having modified the course of that narrative.

Manganelli's hidden "theme" then is literature and its production, and it is present here as an all-embracing metaphor in which literature, in Manganelli's meaning of the word, is represented by death, and the writers who produce literary objects are the dead (and let us not forget that "the gods" too are dead). This metaphorical mirror-image of literary production is what connects the apparently disparate texts in the book. Having rather baldly stated the basic terms of this metaphor we can now briefly consider the individual texts within this interpretation. However, I do not wish to consider this reading in too much detail because it risks being rather too reductive a treatment of such a complex work, since Manganelli maintains a careful brinkmanship and feedback between the different layers of the text. Thus, for example, while the gods may be thought of as writers some of the time, they are also often "only" gods as well.

The theme of death first assumes its metaphorical aspect in "Ignominy", but the notion of the writer's powers of invention and ordering (in both meanings of the word) is strongly present in the first text. In "A King", the monarch appears supremely in control, ensconced in his castle composed of language. Themes from the manifesto are referred to when he explains that, "When I began to create the royal palace — and particularly the ruins — I built them in the hope that this simulation of history would attract beings that were unaware of my duplicity." Likewise, his meditations on the status of his subjects lead him to question his powers: "are these then the options for kingliness — nothingness or dissimulation?" Something outside his invention has made its presence known: the being with the ocarina, who is indifferent to all the king's efforts and who ignores all his attempts at communication (cf. the "Disquisition"). More importantly, this being is supremely indifferent to its *own* efforts, and everything the king has created begins to seem worthless to him, or beside the point. In "Simulations" a similar tale is told, a fantastic hyperbole of invention gradually gives way to the protagonist's decline and eventual realisation of his futility when faced with an imperfectly formed child. This parable reads in part rather like a half-apologetic reprise of the first paragraph of "Literature as Deception", but both of the seemingly insignificant figures who bring the book's first two texts to such deflationary conclusions in fact appear to personify aspects of their respective narrators, a dawning awareness of their true situation "of being alive and of being dead" as "Ignominy" later puts it, and of the inadequacy of what they have produced. Literature is an *adynaton* according to the manifesto, a categorical impossibility.

The subject of death is ever-present in "Reincarnations", and this is a text in whose outrageously complex travesty of a plot I suspect one can see Manganelli's rejection of any form of literature based upon history, narrative (in its usual meaning), psychology or even philosophy. We should read it perhaps with this statement from the manifesto in mind: "... the writer lives in a state of discontinuous contemporaneity with himself. Thus neither historical events nor the safeguards of literary narrative give us access to literature, but only the act of precisely shaping the language within which literature finds its structure." All of these initial texts are open to more detailed reinterpretation in relation to those that follow, for example, what is one to make of the "mother" in "Simulations", whose narrator reads the classics while still in her womb?

Halfway through the book, with "Ignominy", the writer's situation is considered with some precision: he is dead, in some respects, but trapped in an ignominious limbo of the "not here" and faced with an impossible task, a void to be filled — a needle's eye that must be passed through in order to gain access to somewhere unspecified, a "beyond" that is more literary than theological. Having not yet passed through the biblical eye he is not truly dead, for "no one can be a corpse" in the "not here" although there are some who are able to take on the appearance of being one. The various "deaths" the aspirant may have undergone even to reach this point are duly considered. For example, he can attempt to "become a corpse" by his own efforts, in other words by suicide, which explains the positive light in which this option is viewed throughout the book, in the previous text in particular. Once "dead", do such persons wish to be discovered? Only by the "impossible reader" from the manifesto, who is able to negotiate a supremely difficult literary object that has been constructed for reasons that are incomprehensible to everyone but him: "a situation that is so intimidating that only the person they have in mind — strangely enough — would be able to track them down, a filter that blocks out everyone, except — who? Let us say someone who may have a taste for darkness and the emptiness of place. But if such a person should fail to arrive, what would it mean then?" Perhaps that he is not up to the task? Or he may have sought out this place in order to find somewhere "comfortable … to hide" since there is no place more conducive than the "not here" for indulging in self-delusion.

And if it was not suicide then perhaps he was murdered — certain circumstances have expelled him from ordinary life into the "not here" — or else his death was caused by something insignificant, in which case his productions risk being only feeble and inconsequential, and the symptom of the paucity of his output will be the loss of his "understanding that [he is] dead". The text then becomes highly ironic, and considers the sorry state of those in the "not here" who believe themselves to have attained the state they desired, "those all too-numerous great writers" of the manifesto, who "find themselves at such a distance from one another that there is no way they can be compared, and accordingly they each acquire a kind of spurious dignity that is more treacherous and humiliating than any kind of derision." Despite the reputation that such a writer may possess in the "here", in the "not here" he tends to suffer from "a general air of worthlessness … an infection of worthlessness which prevents him from making a detailed inventory of his own particular revolting indecency". After all, he has chosen this path "when it was completely up to him to manage his self-awareness of the worthlessness of being alive", and so it is not at all unexpected that he should resort "to the awkward business of self-justification".

Towards the end of the text the meaning of the title is clarified when the narrator's situation is characterised as the "ignominy of being alive and of being dead, [which] forces us to dream up these tiresome deceptions — but does our shame not have its accomplices?" This is perhaps a situation akin to Beckett's "Not to want to say, not to know what you want to say, not to be able to say what you think you want to say, and never to stop saying [it]" (*Molloy*). Or more simply a writer resigned to his own failure, but determined to carry on regardless, even if all the plaudits of his "accomplices" (critics, academics etc.) are not able to suppress his own awareness of his bad faith, his "worthlessness". Manganelli, however, does not accept either of these solutions, whatever the accomplices' opinions might be, and the penultimate paragraph of "Ignominy" proposes another solution altogether, and one that is equally unreasonable. It is this project of creating a "real, and truly homicidal murderer" that we presume is being attempted in this book, and which is addressed to those Manganelli hopes may collaborate on such a solution: *To Those Gods Beyond*.

"An Impossible Love" is perhaps the most elegant literary text here, in which Hamlet and the Princess of Clèves ruminate on the imminent destruction of their worlds and wish for a death that is even more impossible for them, as fictional characters, than is their love. Whereas the previous text considered the position of the *dishonest* writer, conscious of his compromises but who carries on regardless for motives that seem disreputable, "An Impossible Love" considers the opposite case, the *honest* failures.

Here, in their fictional universes, three principal characters find themselves marooned, and in this second-degree reality the role of the gods is clear, because the *creators* of these characters are truly dead. William Shakespeare and Madame de La Fayette are no more, and their universes are teetering on the point of extinction. The princess confirms this: "death no longer knows how to preserve us," but perhaps Manganelli himself is assuming this role, since in the blurb for the first edition of this book he tells us that it is by "immortalising the past" and simultaneously "archaicising the future" that something contemporary can be made. In these simulated universes, meanwhile, where even water can fracture, for the first time two different types of death can be distinguished: "authentic" and "emblematic". The true gods (those oxymorons) have now suffered the first of these twice over, or both of them once, depending on how one looks at it; the ghost endlessly enacts the second (thereby becoming "immortal" by accident), while Hamlet and the princess yearn for the first type of death but are permitted only the second, to *die on stage* in a simulation (even those dwelling at Colombelles resemble actors, we discover, since the princess's father dies on more than one occasion).

These characters are treated with some affection by Manganelli, as opposed to the distaste he showed for various of those in the previous text. One can hazard a few interpretations. Both Hamlet and the princess are typecast as versions of themselves, so that in Hamlet we see something like the figure of a romantic poet, hopelessly outdated, and in the princess perhaps a psychological novelist, musing over the ever more arcane subtleties of her "no" in some sort of "Hampstead novel". So if Hamlet is a stand-in for the emotions and the princess for intellect, what then is the role of the ghost?

We first discover him on the battlements of Elsinore: "a phantasm, a poor wretch, a non-thing". He is "winking at one of his own kind", a phrase that recalls one from the previous text in which the narrator's "pointless winking, this mawkish, flirtatious and provocative posturing from within the shroud of non-existence appears only to be a sort of indiscretion". Manganelli shows a particular sympathy for this "penetrable" personage who seemingly plays the role of a hack writer (the literary equivalent of a "ham actor"). Hamlet informs us: "the ghost of my father is not on the side of death. Quite the contrary. As you have clearly understood, he is one of the others." So who are these "others", the "unnaturals" or "subterraneans"? They are perhaps writers grubbing a crust on the fringes of literary existence, roguish miscreants with the air of "a dubious mariner ever on the look-out for illicit gains and profitable schemes". The ghost's usual scam is plagiarism, judging from the fact that he steals the "identity" of those on the verge of death, a necessity forced upon him because he himself is "shorn of death, and destiny." He is but one of a numberless horde: "There is no vein or fissure … that does not crawl with us". (The recurrence of fissures, flaws, rifts and cracks is a notable part of the literary sub-text throughout this book.) And he is well aware of his situation, which he describes with a certain rueful relish:

"Our situation is rather odd since it casts us in a tragic role, which is all the more grandiose as it is clearly quite useless. The specific nature of our condition derives from the fact that we simply do not acknowledge death. All our mishaps, all our troubles, all our pitiful and pitiable perversions which make us everywhere repugnant and altogether wretched, all of these proceed from this condition of immortality."

Immortality here means the impossibility of dying and thus of ever becoming a maker of literary objects. But the foundering of the literary worlds the ghost inhabits is not something to be taken too seriously: "I should move on, maybe learn another trade, something a little more respectable and less demanding."

In the collapsing realities of "An Impossible Love" only the ghost's appeals to certain beings beyond offer a literal glimmer of hope. Who are they? The "other gods" of the book's title perhaps (the Italian "*ulteriori*" of the title means both "other" and "beyond", or "outside"), or is this the "unique being", whom the princess complains is stealing into their world, Manganelli himself? The ghost describes him as "one who has some authority in our world and who has, we suspect, some knowledge, perhaps only a glimpse, of a world to come". If this is Manganelli many years hence then the gods will already have met their Nietzschean fate, just like Shakespeare and La Fayette, and Manganelli here seems to be celebrating the fact that literature has been stripped of at least some of the metaphysical roles with which it has been so unaccountably lumbered, since he envisages a literature with no role but its own creation. Thus the gods, being dead, are writers too, who in Manganelli's universe must create this everything, including themselves, and survive without either believers or worshippers (as in the text that follows, the "Disquisition") but be "for readers who are indeterminate, about to be born, destined not to be born, already born or already dead; even for impossible readers." A difficult existence.

Can the gods survive when no one believes in them? And why should anyone worship beings which act so capriciously and with such malice? In the "Disquisition" these questions find their equivalent in an old conundrum: why write "difficult" literature that "ordinary people" find impossible to understand? This is a particular problem for avant-garde writers with leftist politics (and thus for several of those in Gruppo 63): can there be a modernist form of literature that also communicates with "the people"? Manganelli exactly reverses this question to ask: "Why should the dead feel obliged to communicate with the living?" In the "Disquisition" it is the people who are endlessly pestering the dead to explain themselves. As Manganelli puts it in the manifesto: "… the thought of being asked to explain 'What is it you want to say?' fills him [the writer] with complete horror." No wonder the dead shrink from such contact.

Manganelli's critique of his fellow writers in the "Disquisition" is unstinting: "we cannot rule out the possibility that death makes its unfortunate sufferers stupid", and elsewhere they are "deaf or louts". The note about "Vagabond types" who are "always leaning at an angle" is also surely a description of the vacillations of Manganelli's Marxist "left-leaning" fellow-travellers?

We are unaware of whether this reading of *To Those Gods Beyond* has been proposed previously, and accept that it may seem based on somewhat subjective foundations, although the chronology of when these texts were written does offer evidence that is at least suggestive.

The first to be written and published was the "Disquisition",[1] which is unsurprising given its different form, being divided into sections and so forth. It appears to have been written as a stand-alone work and only later did Manganelli adapt its central metaphor to underpin the texts that were to precede it in this book. In the meantime he had written the manifesto[2] which would provide its theoretical trajectory. The "Disquisition" and the manifesto have a number of quite similar passages in which "the dead" take the place of "the writer". For example:

> Some of them say: "The dead are set apart from history, *ergo*, apart from art and morality; they have no knowledge of dialectics, and perhaps lack any language. Untouched by any moral scruples they are dysfunctional, uneducated, even perverse." Others believe that "those who are now dead did not, even when alive, inhabit history; rather it was prehistory, something beyond reason, irrational, superstitious and savage. Therefore the dead are not, and cannot possibly be other than behind the times. As for dallying in retrospective repartee with them, might they not be victims or murderers, and thus delay, even if only for a moment, the forward progress of History?" They may add: "We assume the language of the dead cannot have for its object anything but the dead themselves; therefore, it cannot be understood, and so we judge it to be meaningless." ("Disquisition")

> Wrapped up in its convolutions, trapped within the sphere of his language, the writer is neither a contemporary to events, which are unable to conform to a chronology compatible with his biography, nor even to those of other writers with whom he co-exists, except when they too are engaged with the very same language: a situation that is metaphysical rather than historical. It also happens that, through the coercive demands of language, and the acute instability and natural infidelity of the worldly, the writer lives in a state of discontinuous contemporaneity with himself. Thus neither historical events nor the safeguards of literary narrative give us access to

literature, but only the act of precisely shaping the language within which literature finds its structure. (Manifesto)

In *To Those Gods Beyond* and in his manifesto, Manganelli explicitly rejects the literary preoccupations of most of his contemporaries, and of ours too. For him literature is both the fate and fête of language, and it cannot be purposed into representing anything "real", as the final sentence of the citation above makes clear. In this book at least, literature is presented as principally representing not the world so much as the relationship that language and literature have with the world, and just as the "Disquisition" inverted the relation between literature and its supposed audience, the book as a whole inverts the relation between language and the supposed world.

In the "Disquisition" Manganelli asks "if Language has an intimate relationship with the world, or rather, as some would prefer, is the world itself...": such an equivalence, which is frequently asserted in the manifesto, makes literature into something all-consuming and "ominously omnivorous". Its matter, the artifices of language, must therefore be celebrated as something primal and originary, in the same way as, say, the equations of pure mathematics, and indeed it has its own equivalent of such equations — the figures of speech in which Manganelli so delighted. When these figures are ordered according to certain arbitrary codes, either compulsory (e.g. syntax) or voluntary (such as heraldry), language is transformed into literature, an independent "structure" whose connection to what it supposedly describes is thus at least partly arbitrary and certainly not to be trusted. Yet when simultaneously directed and given its head this literary language is able to attain a certain congruency or alignment with the world, while neither describing nor representing it. Instead it simulates and reflects it in a conscious dissimulation which, in the end, is not so different from "being alive

[and] being dead" because it can never be more than an approximation, and one to whose imperfections Manganelli is decidedly reluctant to resign himself.

Near the end of the manifesto he asserts that: "Literature organises itself as a pseudo-theology, in which a whole universe is celebrated". There are many "gods" in this theology, and "beyond" one god, or even inside it, another god is always to be found *ad infinitum*; there are meanings within meanings and all of them are equally true and equally false. The tertiary "theme", of congruence rather than representation, comes to us by way of a demonstration: the book itself reflecting on itself, *ad infinitum,* by means of an over-arching and highly ironic metaphor. For Manganelli it seems that the world is no more than this, a metaphor, or more prosaically, a mechanism whose main, and perhaps sole function is to supply literature with the figurative components it will utilise to fulfil its impossible aim — that of fully representing itself. This is the task Manganelli has set himself, to "try, as one who is dead, to find the right way through" ("Ignominy").

The final sentence of *To Those Gods Beyond* almost says as much: "Some hint of this dialogue is already in the air, a hilarity at once secret and circumspect, a way of speaking through conspiratorial enigmas." John Walker notes that the "Disquisition" was written soon after the publication of Manganelli's first book, *Hilarotragoedia.*

NOTES

1. It was first published in the journal *Menabò* in 1965.
2. Published in 1967, five years before *Agli dèi ulteriori* (*To Those Gods Beyond*).

BLURB TO THE FIRST EDITION

Giorgio Manganelli

●

Manganelli was well known for writing his own blurbs, and overleaf is the one he wrote for this book when it was first published by Einaudi in 1972. It is worth noting that the Avernese language mentioned would apply to the region around Avernus, the volcanic crater near Naples which the Romans took to be the entrance to the underworld and whose name quickly came to signify the underworld in general. And also that the letter "h" is silent in Italian.

J.W.

The anecdotes, accumulations of verbs and sounds and marks on paper which are collected here, and which the reader has acquired in appreciation of the ambiguous seduction of the dust-wrapper, suffer from a serious inadequacy which it would be pointless to excuse since it is an essential part of their character. In fact, what is presented in this work is simply a series of transcriptions or translations from a variety of foreign languages, and the Italian is nothing but a linguistic vehicle for carrying the meaning, like the Swahili which so many readers use to communicate with their superiors, or Wolof, which they employ to keep in touch with their inner nature, be it mental or physical.

It is obvious, for example, that the "Disquisition on the Difficulty of Communicating with the Dead" conceals sections written in Avernese — the mother tongue of the fourth story — while the third text presupposes a language that is derived from it, a kind of Neo-Avernese: this latter, one way or another and as everyone must know, is of necessity the language of the future, and who can doubt that in some way even a collector of dust-wrappers must vaguely understand that fact? The majority of the phonemes here were put together in a leisurely manner one summer in Catalonia by a carefree minor nobleman muttering away to himself while sitting astride a derelict old shadow disguised as a warhorse. He promptly left them behind one hurricane-lashed evening in the deserted farm where he had found shelter from the tender fury of the rain, only for them to be rediscovered years later by a bankrupt trader in antiques, and end up in the first of the texts presented here. Appended to that text, which is no more than a veritable "corpus of quotations", are pages from the same period that were purchased from a similar pedlar who, even though he dressed in black and claimed he was a Nordic academic, sounded half Flemish and half Baltic to our ears. It would be wrong to say that the fifth tale revives the presumed language of this protagonist, because for this text all we have is a transcription made at a much later date and certainly revised by its co-authors, and from a language which it seems reasonable to suppose is still to be discovered. Consequently this translated text is only really able to function backwards, by archaicising the future while simultaneously immortalising the past, and thereby producing something that is contemporary.

Because this book is an assemblage of various letters of the alphabet, some perhaps of rather base extraction, which have been brought together more out of fear that they will ultimately be dispersed than out of pure love, it is perhaps incumbent on the compiler to indicate which of these letters, in his opinion — the product of judgement and the decorum of good manners — deserve a certain indulgence. Our preference, which is close to passion, is for the letter *h*: solitary, ectoplasmic, a muffled blessing and a phonetic nothing, whose lower-case form resembles the warhorse destined to carry us as far as the gateway to the capital, H, which in its great silence promises comfort at last.

ATLAS ANTI-CLASSICS

For a complete listing of all titles available from Atlas Press
and the London Institute of 'Pataphysics see our online catalogue at:
www.atlaspress.co.uk
To receive automatic notification of new publications
sign on to the emailing list at this website.
Atlas Press, 27 Old Gloucester st., London WC1N 3XX
Trade distribution UK: www.turnaround-uk.com; USA: www.artbook.com